SHIFTING SANDS

Ruth's father tells her that he has taken on Paul as a business partner, and whilst being obliged to co-operate with him, Ruth's reaction is to feel a deep distrust for a man she hardly knows. However, she comes to trust him and love him as they work together to track down her cousin Melanie, who has disappeared. Then Paul saves Ruth's life at serious cost to himself . . . just as they finally locate Melanie who is in great danger . . .

Books by Shelagh Fenton
in the Linford Romance Library:

THE HOUSE IN THE TREES

WL

SHELAGH FENTON

◆

SHIFTING SANDS

Complete and Unabridged

LINFORD
Leicester

First published in Great Britain in 2003

First Linford Edition
published 2009

British Library CIP Data

Fenton, Shelagh.
   Shifting sands - - (Linford romance library)
   1. Executives- -Fiction. 2. Missing persons- -
   Investigation- -Fiction. 3. Romantic suspense
   novels. 4. Large type books.
   I. Title II. Series
   823.9′2–dc22

   ISBN 978–1–84782–866–8

Published by
F. A. Thorpe (Publishing)
Anstey, Leicestershire

Set by Words & Graphics Ltd.
Anstey, Leicestershire
Printed and bound in Great Britain by
T. J. International Ltd., Padstow, Cornwall

This book is printed on acid-free paper

1

Paul Mackay arrived for petrol just as Ruth Tamworth was struggling off the garage forecourt with her suitcases. She greeted him awkwardly, feeling hot and dishevelled.

'What's happened to your car?' he asked.

'The engine's on the blink. Stan's looking into it. He wanted me to wait for the taxi to return from the school run, but there's such a lot to do this evening, I decided to catch the bus.'

'I'm glad I arrived at the right moment. Hop in and I'll stack your gear in the back.'

He swung Ruth's bags into the boot, filled up with petrol, and slipped into the driver's seat.

'Surely you need your car for tomorrow.'

His blue eyes looked troubled.

'Stan's going to work late to have it ready in time.'

'How does it feel then to be back in Harleywell after six months away?'

'I'm only really passing through. Tomorrow I go to Laitheham for a week and as soon as Dad's finalised his plans, I'll be moving there.'

'But you're staying on at your old job until then?'

Ruth nodded. She liked her job in Harleywell. All the same, she'd enjoyed this six months secondment the chain had offered her in Leeds, the chance to gain experience as stand-in manageress at their boutique there. Now she was ready to take on running something herself.

'Your father told you our news, I imagine,' Paul commented as they came in sight of their house.

'That you've gone into partnership with him? Yes, Dad put me in the picture a couple of days ago.'

Ruth smoothed down her skirt and straightened the clip holding up her long hair.

'You disapprove!'

'Of course I don't disapprove.'

She was uneasy, though. Everybody liked Paul and he was clearly a competent businessman. In just two years he'd changed his aunt's traditional gift shop in Harleywell into a craft centre that brought in customers from miles around. However, Dad was risking a big chunk of his savings in this new Laitheham venture, and for things that mattered, Paul Mackay was a man they hardly knew. He'd only been actually resident in Harleywell for less than a year.

'It makes good business sense,' Paul pointed out. 'Your father wanted a partner for his Laitheham project, and I've inherited a small bit of capital from my grandfather.'

'But you've completely changed the original project.'

'Not much. Not really.'

'Dad says there's going to be a sizeable craft element in the new shop, not just the flowers.'

Their plan, or Dad's plan, had been

for a simple flower shop. Paul had persuaded him to add studio craft items, like those he'd had such success with in Harleywell. Ruth rubbed the end of her nose anxiously. Flowers and floristry were what she understood. Studio crafts, such as weaving and pottery were another world.

'Flowers are halfway to craft items nowadays, what with dried arrangements and pot plants,' Paul pointed out.

'It depends how you look at it.'

'I'll tell you how I see it later.'

Paul pulled off into their drive. Dad came bustling out and Ruth found herself explaining about her car all over again. As she was talking, Mrs Morris from across the road ran across and thrust a letter into Ruth's hand.

'The postie left this with us by mistake.'

After a quick glance at the envelope, Ruth shoved it in the outside pocket of her bag as Paul unloaded her suitcases and took them into the house.

'I put them in your room. I hope that was OK,' he said when he returned.

'Fine, thanks.'

Yet somehow she felt put out at the way he'd made himself at home, as though he lived here and she was the visitor. He'd looked her up a couple of times in Leeds to bring her vegetables from Dad's garden, passing through on his way to buying trips farther north. Both men liked gardening and Paul now helped Dad with the heavier work. With that and the swimming pool committee they had a lot in common. All the same, Ruth hadn't realised they'd got so close while she'd been away.

For example, Paul had made over their tiny front garden into a patio with tubs, a typical Paul design of white and grey, set out in neat straight lines, cool and subtle. He'd left the enormous, honey-scented rose sprawling against the house wall, though, Ruth noticed. They'd had one just like it at their house in Laitheham when she was a child.

Dad had gathered some of the huge white floppy roses and stuffed them in a tall vase in the lobby, she noticed when they went indoors.

'I can't manage a proper display like you, lass,' he remarked, 'but I thought you'd like the scent of them.'

Ruth buried her nose in the flowers. The fragrance was overpowering and roused a thousand memories, bitter-sweet, some of them. Last time she'd been in Laitheham, three years ago, the rose there had been in full bloom. A happy omen, she'd thought, unaware that her happiness was built on sand.

The kettle whistling in the kitchen interrupted her thoughts. Paul strode in ahead of her and poured the water into the teapot.

'I'll do the rest,' Ruth told him.

Paul hesitated, then nodded and returned to the lounge. Ruth saw him pick up a stack of papers, to do with either the new swimming pool or with the Laitheham shop, no doubt. He and Dad worked well together. If only everything wasn't rushing ahead so fast.

When the phone rang, Ruth answered it. It wasn't good news. Stan at the garage said her car needed a new condenser, and because it was an old model he couldn't take delivery of a spare until next week. So how was she going to travel to Laitheham tomorrow for the start of her one-week course? Since his heart attack, Dad no longer ran his own car.

Ruth rang the local coach company immediately, but they were already fully booked. That left the train from Birmingham to Carlisle.

Dad looked worried when she told him the change of plan.

'How do you get to Birmingham?' he asked.

'The early-morning London bus stops there, Dad.'

'And from Carlisle to Laitheham?'

'There's still a bus service, I think.'

Thirty miles, it would be, up hill, down dale! Hopefully the last bus didn't depart before her train arrived in

Carlisle. If it did, she'd just have to take a night's lodging and hope the first bus on Saturday would get her to Laitheham early enough to enrol on her course, or there was car hire. Ruth rubbed her chin, wondering. The two men had their heads together and Ruth saw Dad pat Paul's hand.

'I could take you to Laitheham tomorrow,' Paul volunteered. 'I was going up to Cumbria on a buying trip next week anyway. I can bring it forward.'

'There's no need. I'll be fine on the train.'

'Rail travel can be very expensive for last-minute bookers,' Paul pointed out, 'in addition to two bus journeys. It makes better business sense for me to drive you there.'

Ruth stifled a sharp answer. It was true that the new business was paying her expenses for this course, but she wasn't freight to be shipped around as cheaply as possible.

'I'll foot the extra bills myself,' she

said stiffly. 'After all, it's my fault. I must have neglected my car for it to have broken down suddenly like this.'

'Nonsense, lass. Sometimes cars just pack up. It'd be a real opportunity,' Dad continued, 'for the two of you to look at any shop premises in Laitheham together.'

'I'd be best to do this course before embarking on anything, Dad.'

The course was all about Laitheham as a commercial centre, and about business décor, things Ruth felt she knew little about.

'Learn on the hoof's my motto. That's how I built up my wagon business and you've always had your feet firmly on the ground,' her dad went on.

Dad must have forgotten her engagement! Ruth turned away to hide a stupid blush.

'We could look at premises, together,' Paul agreed.

'There you are, then, Ruthie, it's settled!'

Dad grinned as though he'd won a prize, and Ruth could see there was no arguing with the plan. So much for any free time during the course, if there was going to be any free time, that is. Everything had been arranged in such a rush, Ruth had only a hazy idea of what she'd let herself in for. Dad had seen the advert, wheedled her a place on the course, then rung her with the news.

'It was meant to be,' he'd insisted, 'coming straight after you'd finished your six months in Leeds.'

That evening, Ruth studied the course prospectus and started to have cold feet. It looked very technical. There might be a bit of free time, though, of an evening, especially since as a late booking she didn't have live-in accommodation at Laitheham Hall.

Two days were marked as free time for familiarisation studies, but nothing explained what that meant. Tramping the fells, perhaps, or beachcombing in Laitheham Bay? Should she take her trail boots with her? She might need something smart, as well, if Paul wanted them to eat out somewhere special. With a sigh, Ruth decided to re-do the small suitcase she'd brought home ready packed for Laitheham. In Leeds, she'd packed her trail boots wrapped in an old newspaper she'd found in her flat there. After now repacking the boots in a canvas bag, Ruth flicked through the newspaper, reliving the warm, cosmopolitan Leeds atmosphere, so different from staid, stand-offish Harleywell.

The centre spread was a regular candid camera spot. Ruth caught her breath as one picture leaped out at her. LOCAL BUSINESSMAN RELAXES was the caption, and the picture was of Paul Mackay.

Did Paul do business in Leeds? If so, he'd never mentioned it the couple of times he'd called on her there. Ruth checked the date. The newspaper was two years old and as she looked closer, the photo showed a man very different from the open, straightforward Paul

Mackay she knew.

Was the photo taken at a nightclub or at a private party? The caption didn't say and the picture was close-cropped. Who was the girl, Ruth wondered. A business contact? She looked about sixteen and had next to nothing on. Should she show the picture to Dad?

In the end Ruth decided not to. He was old-fashioned in his ideas and it might unsettle him. The partnership with Paul was signed and sealed. There was no going back on it, so Dad needed to feel confident in his new partner. And Paul's private life was, of course, nothing to do with them, especially from two years ago.

She tore out the cutting and filed it with other newspaper clippings she'd kept under the letters in her desk drawer. She caught sight of another newspaper shot she hadn't looked at for a long while now. For the first time she noticed how Paul looked a little bit like Brian.

2

Next day they travelled up the motor-way without talking. Paul seemed withdrawn and Ruth couldn't help suspecting he felt irritated at being pressured into changing his plans to bring her north today. The newspaper item she'd seen last night was another barrier.

The silence was covered by the radio, music they both liked, mixed with a medley of news. One item, about two women risking their lives to save a child from drowning stirred troubled memories of Ruth's mum's death in a boating accident. If Mum hadn't died Dad might never have left Laitheham. Together they might have struggled on through the lean years.

'Jo says the swimming pool fund is ahead of schedule,' Paul commented.

Jo! It had been Mr Tamworth before

she went to Leeds, though first names seemed more natural now they were partners, of course.

It was mid-afternoon before they came in sight of the Cumbrian Fells, a jagged azure line across the horizon. Ruth studied the peaks, named each one silently and remembered the last time she'd walked to the summit, heard skylarks trilling there or caught the fleeting red flash of a deer.

They stopped for a snack at a service area. Ruth sipped her coffee, feeling she ought to be making conversation. Paul was college trained, she knew, so perhaps he might give her a few clues about how to tackle her one-week course, but her attention kept straying to the distant fells.

'I can see from your face that you're coming home,' Paul remarked with a smile.

'Which route are you taking north from here?'

Paul glanced at his watch.

'We'd do better to stay on the

motorway as far as Carlisle then cut across on the main road west, I think, if you agree.'

'That's fine by me.'

'Is it?'

'Why not?'

'You sounded as though something wasn't quite right.'

'No. It's much quicker than the scenic route.'

'But you looked troubled,' Paul insisted.

'I was only trying to remember how you reach my hotel from that direction,' Ruth prevaricated.

This was a half-truth. The hotel was new, held no memories, which was why she'd chosen it.

'Parkways is near the golf course,' Paul explained, 'up the hill opposite the filling station. I asked Mrs Saunders the way when I rang through to book myself a room.'

'You mean you're staying at Parkways, too?'

'Is that an intrusion?'

Paul shot her a sharp glance.

'Of course not,' Ruth assured him quickly.

It was, though. All the plans she'd had for her free time in Laitheham were starting to ooze away, first because she'd lost her car, then Paul had pressed for them to look at premises together, now this. But she needed to cooperate with Paul.

'I thought we ought to be in contact if we're hoping to view properties together,' Paul remarked.

'I won't have much free time,' Ruth reminded him.

'Me neither. Most days I'll be out on the buying trail. North Cumbria and the Borders is a huge area, with a lot of craft studios.'

'Tell me about them, Paul.'

This was a subject she needed to understand if the simple flower shop she and Dad had planned was now going to stock craft items as well. It was soon clear Paul loved his work. He was still talking when Carlisle came in sight!

'My favourite city,' Paul remarked.

'Mine, too,' Ruth agreed after a while, half-reluctantly.

She traced the familiar skyline, hunting for the square outline of the massive castle and the cathedral above the sea of red-brick terraces. The ancient sentinel of the north harboured raw and confusing memories. She was glad when Paul turned off without actually driving through the city.

'How long did you say it was since you were last in Laitheham?' Paul asked as they headed west.

'Three years.'

'You'll find changes then.'

Early-evening haze was already thick on the sea when they came in sight of Laitheham Bay. The tide was right out and brightly-painted yachts on the brown mud of the little harbour sprawled this way and that, waiting for the sea to return. Ruth wound down her window to gulp in the tangy air and listen to the gulls screaming overhead. Home! Just for a moment it was as though she'd never been away.

Then out of the corner of her eye she caught sight of new buildings on the far side of the harbour, large, white, glaring buildings, not at all in keeping with the squat grey-brown cottages along the harbour wall. Paul turned left by the filling station and the houses vanished from sight, obscured by the tall, Victorian terraces flanking the hill.

From the window of her room at the hotel Ruth could see the new complex quite well. More than one modern building had sprung up. Although she had grown up here and knew the town so well, she could no longer make sense of the jumble of roofs on the main street along the harbour. Dad's former lorry park had grown enormously.

A cool breeze fanned Ruth's cheeks as she stood at her open window. In the distance, the sea moaned insistently. That meant the tide was on the turn. As a child she'd lived by the tides. They gave pattern and shape to the day, a beautiful pattern, until Mum died in the boating accident and she'd discovered the sea and Laitheham could be cruel and treacherous.

This was something she'd rediscovered in a different way two years ago, three years ago, even, when she'd come here with Brian the month they'd got engaged. Even then there had been cracks showing in their relationship.

Below her in the hotel carpark she saw Paul fetching something from his car. Paul was a Nottinghamshire man, yet he loved Laitheham and West Cumbria. That's what had first brought him and Dad close, a shared love of Dad's home town.

Paul noticed her and waved. Ruth waved back and pretended to be studying the view in the other direction, the wide arc of the western fells. Over the road, Laitheham golf course stretched towards them, a green carpet. A track she didn't know skirted the golf course and plunged down towards the harbour. Ruth vowed to walk it while she was here, new memories to drive out the old, unhappy ones.

Paul had phone calls to make and had arranged to meet her downstairs in half an hour. Since Parkways offered only bar snacks of an evening they'd decided to go out for a meal. Ruth had never been out to dinner with Paul before. She showered and changed into the narrow skirt and silky top she'd packed on top of her case.

With five minutes to fill, she decided to have another read of the programme for the course she was starting next day. Hopefully Dad was right, about learning on the hoof. Certainly most of the brochure was 'way over her head. The staff, however, looked approachable. Out of the three tutors only one was a Cumbrian, Janice Enright. Trained abroad, it said, but a Cumbrian who had her own craft centre near Cockermouth.

There was a photograph of her. In spite of a faint, dissatisfied droop to her mouth she was a good-looking woman. Long jade earrings and a dark green sweater set off her flaming red hair perfectly. Unconsciously, Ruth reached up and adjusted the clasp holding up her own rich brown hair, brushed the creases out of her long dark skirt and settled the neckline of her smoke-brown top against her tanned skin. Colour was something she knew all about from her job. This Janice Enright certainly understood how to make it work for her.

Trained abroad, it said. Would all the students barring herself also be college graduates? What if she couldn't keep up with them? There was a grade for the project at the end, and a diploma you could mention on business stationery. What if she failed to make it? Would Paul Mackay call it a waste of money sending her? Would he push Dad to take on someone else instead to run the new shop? Dad would never agree, of course. But it would place a strain on their partnership. She mustn't fail.

Ruth shoved the brochure into her handbag, ready for tomorrow. As she did so she noticed the corner of an envelope peeping out of the outside pocket. It was the letter from Melanie, the one left at Mrs Morris's by mistake. In all the confusion over her changed travel plans she'd forgotten it.

By the time Ruth had read it through several times it was past the hour Paul had arranged to meet her downstairs. She hurried down and found him waiting for her.

'I thought we might walk down and admire the view,' Paul suggested.

'In that case, do you mind if I drop in at my cousin's flat on the way,' Ruth asked, 'just in case she's off duty?'

'Why not give her a ring?'

'Her flat doesn't have a phone, and her work phone is only for emergencies. Her flat's in the old vicarage. It's right on our route.'

'Maybe she'd like to come for a meal with us if she's free.'

Ruth smiled.

'Accepted on her behalf!'

Melanie loved company, new faces,

meals out, anything like that.

However, although Ruth tried the flat bell-push several times, no-one came. In fact the whole of the former vicarage was in darkness. Ruth had brought a postcard with her just in case so she scrawled a message on it and popped it in the letter-box for Flat A.

'Is your cousin expecting you?' Paul asked.

'I did drop her a line from Leeds, but it hadn't reached her when she wrote a letter on Wednesday. I hadn't yet booked the room at Parkways to tell her my address. She'll get in touch when she reads my card.'

'Didn't you say Melanie was a receptionist at one of the hotels? Could we have our meal there?'

'She's at The Highlander.'

Ruth frowned. She didn't want to go to The Highlander with Paul. She didn't want to go to The Highlander at all.

'They usually have a very good dinner menu,' Paul remarked.

'Let's try it then.'

It would look odd if she was to hold back.

'You sound reluctant,' Paul said. 'Will your cousin mind being jumped on at work without warning?'

'Of course not.'

Towering clouds were blowing in from the sea and although it was mid-June and not very late it seemed almost dark when they reached The Highlander. For a moment Ruth thought they'd come to the wrong place when Paul ushered her towards the brightly-lit modern facade.

'I told you to expect changes,' he commented as she hesitated. 'It's under new management.'

The former Smugglers' Inn was still there, as a picturesque bar at the far end. Some of the new décor had low beams and rough walls to tone in with it, but the result lacked character, very different from her last visit three years ago. Ruth swallowed her feelings.

'I'll find out whether Mel's on

Reception before we go through to the restaurant,' she said.

The only person on duty was a part-timer, a newcomer who didn't know any of the other girls. Ruth didn't like to pester a waiter who was hovering in the foyer.

'There's a duty rota that's changed on Friday night,' she told Paul, 'but the new one hasn't gone up yet.'

'We'll try again after our meal,' he suggested.

In the end, however, they didn't eat at The Highlander after all, as the restaurant was fully booked by a coach party. Coach tours in Laitheham! Things really had changed, Ruth realised.

'The changes are our friend,' Paul pointed out.

It was true, of course. Dad had first planned his new shop here because of the tourists who kept the town alive now that the fishing and other family trades had gone. Along the harbour there was another hotel with a restaurant, but that, too, was full.

'Shall we try the chipper?' Paul asked.

'If it's still there.'

'Last time I came it was.'

Last time she'd come it had been, too. Brian had prompted them to go there and they'd stood in the queue, reliving childhood memories, since Brian had also grown up in Laitheham. Friday nights there were always bundles of chips and peas and the race to get them home still hot for Dad who'd always eaten at home with them on Friday nights. No night lorry runs on a Friday had always been his rule.

'Penny for them,' Paul murmured, squeezing Ruth's arm.

'You'd be bored,' she said.

'Try me,' he pressed.

But the queue had moved on and it was their turn to order.

'Let's take our supper out on to the harbour wall, shall we? Out of the wind behind the old lamp housing would be best.'

How well Paul knew Laitheham, as

well as she did. A flock of greedy seagulls followed them. Paul tossed them a chip and was mobbed.

'They'll have them all off you,' Ruth warned with a smile.

When they'd finished their supper they walked out to the end of the harbour wall. The huge rain cloud had disappeared. The tide was rising, a sea of liquid gold beneath the setting sun. They paused to admire the scene.

'This is perfection to me,' Paul commented. 'Such spectacular beauty cheek by jowl with the homeliness of the town.'

Ruth nodded, and Paul pulled her arm through his. For a moment she felt very close to him. Such moments meant next to nothing, however, as she'd learned two years ago with Brian. Ruth manoeuvred her arm free.

'We ought to be getting back to the hotel,' she said. 'I need to sort out my things for the course tomorrow.'

That was, after all, what she'd come here for.

On the way, they called in at The Highlander again. This time no-one was on duty, but the rota was now up, right by the bell. However, Melanie's name wasn't on it. She must be either ill or on holiday this week.

Back in her hotel room Ruth dug out Melanie's letter and reread it. There was no mention of a holiday week coming up, nor of feeling unwell, nor was it a reply to her own note explaining she'd be in Laitheham this week. Clearly their letters had crossed in the post. Though typed, Melanie's letter was signed with her usual fancy calligraphic signature. The paper was thyme-scented, and Ruth recalled Mel loved anything to do with herbs. At the bottom she'd doodled a tiny sage plant, with forget-me-not flowers.

Mel had always been clever with her pencil. She would have had no qualms about this course, in fact Melanie never had butterflies about anything or anyone. That, Ruth recalled, was why Dad, who'd brought her up, worried so much about her, even though Mel thought that at nineteen she was old enough to manage her own life.

Ruth glanced at the time. Should she slip down to Melanie's flat again? Then she'd have something to tell Dad if he rang in the morning. But she decided against it, simply because it was now quite late and she still had the course hand-outs to read.

3

Next morning, Paul gave Ruth a lift out to Laitheham Hall, saying it was on his way.

'And I'll pick you up again at five,' he said as he dropped her off.

Then he drove off too quickly for Ruth to protest. Ruffled, she crossed the road and walked up the splendid beech avenue to the Hall. There was a perfectly good bus service and she had intended to use it. Paul had his own programme and she had hers.

This evening, for example, she'd planned to stay on the bus down into town and slip round to Mel's flat again, since she'd received no message from her yet. Time was short, with only a week to fit everything in. Her irritation eased, however, as she came in sight of the soothing, solid grey eighteenth-century mansion. Dad had worked for the family here before he'd set up on his own. Now the local authority used it as a course centre.

Registration was in the former stables. Ruth ran her eye down the list of other students on the course. They all had letters after their names. It looked like she had a hard week ahead of her.

Day One was Orientation Day, a trip round West Cumbria and the northern fells, and their tutor for the day was Janice Enright, the Cumbrian woman Ruth had noticed in the brochure. The photo did her less than justice. She was extremely attractive, with an eye-catching, big-city style.

As they all clambered out of the minibus at the end of the day she came across to Ruth.

'You seem to know this area inside-out already,' she commented.

'I lived in Laitheham as a child.'

'When did you move away?'

'When I was fourteen,' Ruth began, but before she could tell more, Paul arrived to pick her up.

At the sound of a car on the gravel, Janice turned round. Her eyes widened, and as Paul came to a halt she walked across to him.

'This is a surprise, Paul!' she exclaimed.

'For me, too,' he replied. 'I've just dropped by to give Ruth a lift back into Laitheham.'

He climbed out of his car, looking, Ruth noticed, a bit uncomfortable.

'You two know each other then?'

Janice turned back to Ruth with a smile.

'It's Ruth's father I'm in partnership with for this Laitheham venture I told you about. Ruth's going to run the outfit for us,' Paul was saying.

'That's why I'm doing this course,' Ruth explained. 'I've never actually been in sole charge of a retail outlet on my own before.'

'Well done, stretching your wings.'

Janice's smile was warm, but Ruth felt she was sizing her up, and figuring her as green and inadequate. Why go telling people you had no experience when they might not need to know?

'I did a business course before I set up on my own,' Janice said. 'That's where I first met Paul.'

She grinned at him and linked her arm through his. Paul returned her grin, but pulled his arm away.

'What are you doing here at the Hall, Jan?' he asked.

'Tutoring on the course, darling. Sharing my expertise.'

'I never knew you did teaching work,' Paul replied.

'It brings in a few extra pennies and makes a change from being stuck in the Centre day in, day out.'

'Janice has her own crafts and garden centre,' Paul explained, 'near Cockermouth.'

Cockermouth! Wasn't that where Paul said he sometimes stayed when he was in the area? Ruth felt suddenly very in the way!

'Where are you putting up this time,

Paul?' Janice asked.

'At Parkways. We're both there.'

'Lovely views. I do the flowers there. But isn't it breakfast only?'

'That's right.'

'Well, why don't the two of you follow me home and I'll give you something to eat?'

Paul glanced at Ruth. She nodded her assent. What else could she do?

'That's fine,' Paul accepted for them both.

'Pot luck,' Janice warned, 'and you'll have to put up with my kids.'

She laughed, patting Paul's shoulder, as though at some shared joke.

'I'll berth the minibus and fetch my car,' she said.

'You are actually happy with the arrangement, aren't you, Ruth?' Paul checked as soon as Janice was out of earshot.

She wasn't, not really. She wanted to return to Parkways and see if there was a message from Melanie, or try her flat again, but she was here with a job to do, and Janice Enright was part of that job. She wasn't only a tutor on the course and Paul's friend, but also a supplier of craft items. Dad had advised her to take every opportunity to meet local people in the trade.

The kids, she discovered on arrival at Janice's, were twins in their mid-teens, Emma and Tim. Either Janice had married very young or she looked much younger than her years. Both youngsters had their mother's flaming red hair and creamy skin. Though only fifteen, their manners were adult and sophisticated, like their clothes. They called Paul by his first name and seemed to get on quite well with him.

Given that the meal Janice had presented them with was pot luck, Ruth wondered what sumptuous banquet Janice could serve if she had time to prepare. As to Janice's craft and garden centre — it was stunning. No wonder they used Janice for a tutor on this course.

Afterwards, Janice served coffee on the patio. The conversation had only just begun, when Ruth wondered if she ought to ring through to Parkways and leave a message for Mel, just in case she tried to contact her.

'How do you propose using your free time from the course?' Janice asked, making an effort to bring Ruth into the conversation.

'Exactly as the brochure recommends,' Ruth replied solemnly, but added, tongue-in-cheek, 'getting to know the area.'

Janice smiled.

'You know it inside-out already!'

'There are a lot of changes,' Ruth pointed out more seriously, 'and I'm hoping to fit in a few visits to old haunts with my cousin, too.'

'You've still got relatives in the area?'

'No resident relatives,' she explained, 'but my cousin's working as a temp at The Highlander.'

'What's her name? Perhaps I know her.'

'Melanie. Melanie Bland.'

Just for a moment Ruth thought she

noticed an odd look flicker in Janice's eyes.

'I think I have met her,' she replied. 'Skinny little lass with long black hair. Looks like an actress or a yoga type.'

'Yes, that's Melanie,' Ruth agreed, though it was a sharp way of describing her cousin's striking and unusual looks. 'She does do yoga. She says it helps her migraine.'

'I remember now. She told me she had migraines. She came for a feverfew plant and we had a chat about it. I suppose someone must have recommended the herb to her.'

'She wouldn't need prompting,' Ruth pointed out. 'Mel's training to be a herbalist herself.'

'I thought you said something about her saving up for a computer course,' Paul commented.

'The computer's just a tool, in Mel's eyes, a means of bringing herbs to people's notice.'

Paul drained his cup just then and stood up.

'Come on, Ruth,' he said. 'We need to be moving.'

'I wanted to show you my barn renovation,' Janice reminded him.

'It'll have to wait, Jan,' he apologised. 'I have to get my partner to Laitheham for an appointment.'

He helped Ruth into her jacket and ushered her towards the door, but Janice held him back for a word in private. Feeling in the way again, Ruth wandered out on to the drive, just in time to see the twins scramble into a large car on the road by the gate. They hadn't popped in to say goodbye, simply headed off without a word. Janice, presumably, must know they were going out. Most things in her life seemed to be planned, under control.

How long had Janice been on her own, Ruth wondered. Apart from explaining that she'd started the garden centre after her husband had been killed in a car crash, Janice hadn't mentioned him. At twenty-eight, Paul was clearly a bit younger than Janice.

Perhaps her husband had been his friend.

There was no doubt that he and Janice were very close, and his easy-going relationship with her children told the same tale. That didn't stop him bending the truth there, though.

'I don't have any appointments and I'm not actually a partner,' Ruth objected to him once they were alone in the car.

'We needed to leave time for you to meet up with your cousin,' he said with a smile. 'That's an appointment. And you're putting your talents into the venture, which is the same as capital.'

'It never occurred to me to do anything else when Dad asked me.'

'That's what I mean. You've got your heart in it.'

He reached across and squeezed her hand. Ruth smiled, pleased, forgetting for a second that Paul was someone who might not always be as straightforward as he seemed. Then she remembered. Did Janice know about his other life in

Leeds? If not, she might be walking into deep unhappiness.

There was no message for Ruth from Melanie at Parkways, so Ruth decided to call round at her flat again.

'Are you sure there's nowhere you can ring her?' Paul asked as he drove her down there.

'Not at her flat or the hotel, like I said. Dad wanted to give her a mobile phone, but she refused. Mel hates gadgets.'

'She likes computers.'

'That's just for her work as a herbalist. What she dislikes is feeling cluttered up with things she doesn't need.'

'The simple life?'

'She is only nineteen.'

Just three years between them, but it was true Ruth did sometimes feel that Melanie was still a child, in some ways. In other ways she acted very independently, sophisticated, even worldly.

There was a light on in the flat at the top of the old vicarage when they arrived and music was playing, too. Ruth rang the bell for Flat A. The music ceased and footsteps came clattering downstairs. But the big, bouncy fair-haired girl who flung open the door wasn't Melanie.

'Oh!' she exclaimed. 'I thought it was Des.'

'I must have pushed the wrong bell by mistake,' Ruth apologised. 'I'm looking for my cousin.'

'Which flat did you want?'

'Flat A.'

'That's my flat. What's your cousin's name?'

'Melanie Bland.'

'No Melanie in these flats, unless it's the girl who was in Flat A before me. The fellow in Flat C on the ground floor knows her. She moved out a few weeks ago.'

'That can't be right. Melanie would have let us know.'

'Did she leave a forwarding address?' Paul asked the girl.

'Not with me. I never met her.'

A car screeched off the road and crunched up the drive.

'There's Des,' the girl squealed. 'If you want to know where your cousin is, ask at Flat C. He knows everything.'

Ruth peered at the almost illegible card for Flat C on the bell-push board.

'He's away at the minute,' the girl added. 'Comes back tomorrow.'

Before Ruth could ask more she slammed the front door behind her and dashed off towards her boyfriend's car.

'That'll be why Mel never got in touch at Parkways,' Ruth commented to Paul. 'She never received my card, nor my letter from Leeds, probably.'

She should have asked the girl about that. What had she done with them? Paul ushered Ruth towards his car in silence.

'I'll slip down for Mel's new address from Flat C tomorrow,' Ruth said.

'Do you think that's wise?'

'Wise? What do you mean?'

'Folk don't always like being hunted out by folk they've known elsewhere, not even their families.'

Paul pulled Ruth's arm through his, but she stepped away from him.

'Some people, maybe,' she retorted sharply, 'but not Melanie. She's not that kind of girl.'

'To me she sounds just that kind of girl. Moves house and doesn't give her new address, refuses a mobile phone.'

'You've never met her. The phone's just not her style.'

'If you say so. It sounds an odd sort of style to me.'

'Not if you know her. She has her little ways, but she's an open book.'

'Perhaps one it takes a clever head to read,' Paul commented.

His words stung Ruth into a silence she couldn't break, confused by her own thoughts.

4

Melanie's mail must be being redirected, Ruth decided, otherwise the new girl in her flat would know her name. She couldn't have got it from the card Ruth herself had left last night. She'd put no name on that, just dropped it in her mail box. But letters through the post must have the name on them. Clearly the girl wasn't receiving Melanie's mail.

Redirected mail meant a new address, an address Melanie hadn't given her family. Why?

That night, Ruth slept badly, allowing her thoughts to stray on to unhappy ground she'd not disturbed for over a year now. How well do you ever really know anyone? But surely her anxieties were nonsense. Melanie wasn't Brian, and she loved Dad, her Uncle Jo, who'd brought her up after her parents divorced. She'd never do anything to

44

worry Dad or cause him pain.

But Paul kept pointing out Melanie had had no idea that Ruth was going to turn up in Laitheham. Her last letter, postmarked Wednesday, gave Flat A, The Old Vicarage as her address, but then it had clearly crossed paths with her own, explaining that she had enrolled on this course. Redirection could be slow, or even fail, especially if the recipient was moving around.

Ruth slept fitfully, and every time she woke the same thoughts kept chasing round her brain. The early midsummer dawn found her still awake. As the light grew stronger Ruth decided to open the heavy curtains and watch the first morning sunlight gilding the rocks out in the bay, just as she used to as a child on those days when Dad was making an early start.

Above the moan of the sea and the shrieking gulls Ruth heard a distant rumble — lorries on the move in the big new transit firm where Dad used to park his three wagons. The sun was fully risen and a bright flash of sunlight on the windscreen picked out each one as it emerged from the secure compound. Ruth counted them. Eight! For Laitheham on a Sunday night that was astonishing.

She decided to go to the early church service before breakfast, like they used to as children. After the service Ruth went to spend a few moments by her mother's memorial stone. Recently, someone had added a low hedge of rosemary. It had to be Melanie. There were flowers in the urn as well, pink daisies and lavender. But the urn was dry. Ruth refilled it, thinking Mel didn't usually neglect flowers or plants. Perhaps she'd left not only her flat but Laitheham.

Footsteps close behind her interrupted Ruth's thoughts. She turned round. It was Paul. They'd parted on cool terms yesterday evening, but the peace of the morning had wiped away the tensions. Melanie's behaviour did look odd, Ruth had to admit it, and Paul probably had his own reasons for suspecting others of leading a double life, something he clearly understood.

'I saw you when I went into church,' Paul said, 'but you looked so preoccupied I thought it was better to stay at the back and leave you to your thoughts.'

Ruth flushed. She'd been thinking about Brian.

Paul started to help her with the flowers. In Harleywell, they often met at church and while she'd been away he'd been giving Dad a lift there on Sundays when the weather was bad.

When they'd tidied the flowers he took time to read the headstone.

'Your mother?' he asked.

'Yes. She died in a boating accident out in the bay. Their engine failed and a gale blew up. She was with her brother. He survived, but Mum couldn't swim.'

'That'll be why Jo's so keen on the new swimming pool.'

Ruth nodded.

'How old were you when your mother died?'

'Fourteen.'

'Is that why your father moved away from Laitheham?'

'Mainly, but the wagon trade here was falling off as well.'

'The new transit firm seems to be a success.'

'There's outsider money in it, though, I imagine, and, of course, the new road has made a big difference.'

Difference, change — that was the story of Laitheham now. That was why Dad had decided to try setting up here again.

The changes in Laitheham and what they meant for business opportunities were the key-point hammered home that day on Ruth's course. Their tutor was a man called Greg who also acted as the development officer for the town.

By tea-time, Ruth was exhausted, but aware, too, that she was the only student on the course with a real-life business project in Laitheham on the stocks, and for all their confident talk, the others had very little local knowledge either. These were her strengths.

Using them was the problem.

Paul had pressed for them to have dinner together. But Ruth found a card in her pigeon-hole at Parkways which said, *Miss Tamworth, Mr Mackay rang to say he's delayed and won't be back till seven thirty.*

Ruth slipped the card in the pocket of her bag and set off at a quick pace into town. It was barely half-past five, which left plenty of time for a word with the tenant in Flat C. That particular flat had an intercom, a new one, Ruth had noticed yesterday. She rang the bell now and waited.

'Who's there?' the disembodied voice asked her.

Ruth gave her name.

'Brian Kane at your service,' the reply came.

Ruth felt herself go white, and her hands started shaking. Her former fiancé had moved away from his previous address in the Midlands, she knew, but never had she imagined he might return to Laitheham. The door opened, and there he was. Ruth found herself struggling for breath.

'Are you OK?' he asked.

He clearly didn't recognise her, and as her commonsense returned, Ruth realised that it wasn't her Brian at all. This man was shorter and more thick-set. Though still tawny, his hair was darker, too. Unlike Brian he slouched, and he mumbled. Because of his work in radio, Brian's voice had always been very sharp and clear, in spite of keeping his local accent.

The superficial similarity was astonishing, though.

'You look terrible,' he said. 'Can I get you a coffee or something?'

'No thanks.'

Ruth couldn't face the idea of being boxed in a room alone with him.

'You need something. I'll fetch you a coffee out here on the bench. The fresh air will do you good.'

'Thank you.'

How rude she'd sounded! Ruth sat down on the bench. That two men should look so alike and have the same name seemed well nigh impossible.

He returned with the coffee.

'You're a better colour now,' he said.

'I skipped lunch,' Ruth admitted. 'Then you gave me a shock. Just for a moment you looked like someone I once knew, a Laitheham man. Your name's the same as well.'

'A double? I like to think that Brendan Kane's unique.'

'Brendan! I thought you said Brian.'

'It may be my cousin that you met. He's a couple of years younger than me, in fact, but as lads, people never could tell us apart.'

'I'm not surprised.'

'His family moved to the Midlands when he was fifteen. He made a career in drama or teaching or something.'

'That's him.'

Brian was a good actor, on stage and off it.

'Why did you look me up?' Brendan asked.

Ruth explained about Melanie.

'Can't help you, sorry. That relationship's in the past. I'm no longer in Miss Bland's confidence.'

Had they been in a relationship? Mel hadn't mentioned him.

'You could try Rudi Leonardson, the manager at The Highlander. He likes to act the tyrant, but he's got a soft centre. He'll help you if he can.'

Ruth frowned.

'Or you could try the Country Club. Melanie often goes there.'

'The new place at the Mansons' old farm?'

They'd heard about it on their course, as an example of an award-winning conversion of a historic building.

'You sound like you used to know the Mansons and their farm.'

Ruth told him about herself, reluctantly, expecting questions about all the business with Brian. He must know his cousin had been engaged to a Laitheham girl who'd moved away. But no questions came.

'I'll take you out to the club if you

like,' he said instead.

Ruth hesitated.

'Pick you up tomorrow evening at eight-thirty,' Brendan pressed.

'I may have met up with Melanie by then.'

'In that case, make it a threesome.'

There was something compelling about his attractive smile, too compelling, too much like Brian's. Ruth held back. What if Melanie didn't fancy a threesome? Maybe Brendan was why she'd left her flat, caught up in a relationship she couldn't manage or didn't want. She might well have suppressed it in her letters home, because Brendan was Brian's cousin.

'Or you can just give me the push,' Brendan said and pulled a face, a humorous face, a little boy's face, yet Ruth felt it masked unhappiness.

'I'll go with you to the Country Club if I haven't met up with Melanie by tomorrow evening,' she agreed.

'And what's the lady's name, and where do I pick her up?' he enquired with a mock bow.

'Ruth Tamworth, and I'm staying at Parkways.'

'Jo Tamworth's daughter, who used to have the wagons?'

'That's right.'

'Great. We'll be able to have a good crack about old times.'

5

Paul, it turned out, had unwittingly chimed in with Ruth's plan, by booking them a table for dinner at The Highlander that evening.

They had a delightful meal, all a far cry from the plain bar meals on offer when Ruth had been here before, a welcome change. She had no wish to remember that last visit. Over the coffee, without going into details, Ruth told Paul that she'd called at Flat C and that she now meant to see if she could secure Melanie's address from the manager at The Highlander, when they'd finished their meal.

'I'll come with you,' Paul said.

They found the manager's office door ajar. Inside, a paunchy man with greying mouse-brown hair was answering the telephone. When he saw them, he waved them to come in and indicated a couple of chairs. Paul ushered Ruth into one as the manager finished his call.

'Rudi Leonardson at your service,' he said. 'How can I help you?'

Though Paul answered him, his eyes stayed on Ruth.

'We're making enquiries,' Paul started, 'about — '

'What enquiries?'

The manager's marked foreign accent seemed suddenly very thick and strong. As footsteps sounded in the corridor outside, Rudi Leonardson went and closed the door. As he brushed past her, Ruth noticed his aftershave was a piercing lavender.

'Now, madam,' he said, turning to Ruth again when he returned, 'what was it you were saying about your friend?'

'I'm here for a week and I was hoping to look up Melanie Bland. She works for you.'

'No, she no longer works for us.'

'What do you mean?' Ruth asked.

In her last letter home Melanie had specifically mentioned her job, and had written that everything was OK at work.

'Miss Bland left our employment about a month ago.'

The manager's features were a mask now, but suspicion flickered in his eyes. Anxiety cooled his wide smile.

'A month ago?' Ruth echoed. 'Did she move to another job?'

The manager said nothing.

'I need Melanie's address to find her, please, Mr Leonardson. Her family is anxious about her. I'm Melanie's cousin, Ruth Tamworth. Melanie lives with my father and me.'

'Normally, of course, I couldn't discuss such matters about an ex-employee, but — ' he began then stopped abruptly.

'What actually happened?' Paul pressed.

'I had no choice,' he said. 'I had to dismiss her.'

'That's ridiculous. Mel's an excellent worker,' Ruth exclaimed.

'Yes, but in a hotel, there are other things, personal involvements. It concerned one of our regulars, a very nice man, a doctor. He was in his fifties, but a young man, if you know what I mean.

No-one could blame Miss Bland for falling in love with him.'

'Falling in love is hardly a crime,' Paul commented.

'It may sound harsh, old-fashioned even, but I had no choice. Her behaviour was so blatant. The gentleman is married and there were complaints from older guests, our regulars.'

Dad, Ruth remembered, had warned Mel about the lack of a proper contract with this job, but the pay had been high and she'd felt it didn't matter. Dad had pointed out it seemed too high for a part-timer and a temp. There had to be a snag. This was clearly it. The manager, as Brendan had remarked, was a tyrant, a law unto himself.

But with a soft centre, Brendan had said. They saw it now as a charming, almost conspiratorial smile lit up his face and he leaned forward in his chair.

'Young people — yes,' he said. 'We love them and their enthusiasms. But me, I have a business to run.'

In spite of his charm, Ruth felt angry

deep inside. Paul tried to restrain her, but she stood up, tight-lipped.

'Could you just give me my cousin's present address, please?'

Mr Leonardson spread his hands.

'Who knows? She had to leave her flat at the Old Vicarage. It's tied to the job. Where she went next, that's up to her.'

'I see.'

Not waiting for Paul, Ruth headed for the door. Outside, she collided with a swarthy waiter she'd noticed last time they came. The impact jolted her bag to the floor. The waiter retrieved it, but not the card that had fallen out under a chair. It was the Parkways telephone message from Paul she'd stuffed in the side pocket earlier, but unaware, Ruth just grabbed her bag and hurried on, eager to escape.

By the reception desk she paused and looked back. Paul was in friendly conversation with the manager, man to man. Without another backward glance, Ruth continued through the foyer and out on to the quayside, where a brisk, cool breeze fanned her flaming cheeks and gave an excuse for tears pricking at her eyes. By the harbour wall Paul caught up with her. He tucked her unresisting arm through his and held her close to him.

'I wheedled this doctor's name and address our of Mr Leonardson,' he explained. 'That's why I hung back.'

'Thank you, Paul.'

She'd misjudged him. Paul squeezed Ruth against him and just for a moment she let herself relax against the comforting support of his arm. But Paul's thoughts were very different from her own. He'd warned her not to go stirring things with Melanie.

'I don't believe all that he said about misconduct,' Ruth told him making her position clear, 'and I won't believe it till I hear it from Melanie herself.'

'Your father once said loyalty was your second name.'

'Dad's always saying silly things.'

'I thought this Dr Roberts might put

us in touch with Melanie. He lives in Carlisle.'

'That's far away to be a regular at The Highlander.'

'I thought the same thing.'

'Most likely he owns a boat in the harbour.'

Otherwise it made little sense, being a regular at The Highlander, thirty miles from his home. From all appearances it was a pleasant enough hotel nowadays, but hardly a place to lure guests on its own account.

Next day was Paul's day for travelling right up into the Scottish Borders. He'd be back too late for dinner. This left Ruth free to take up Brendan's offer to escort her to the Country Club, without too many questions asked.

'Do you know this fellow you're going with?' Paul enquired, but pressed it no further when Ruth said she knew Brendan's family.

Brendan arrived right on time in a van that looked ready for the breaker's yard! It had a surprising turn of speed, however, over the switchback lanes towards the fells. Brendan had called himself a drifter, one of life's idlers.

'Sort of self-employed,' he replied when Ruth pushed the subject.

She had reasons for doing so. If Brendan was self-employed but still allowed to live in the hotel's flat, why was Melanie thrown out when she lost her job? The thought stirred a sudden vivid memory of yesterday's interview with Rudi Leonardson.

At the time Ruth hadn't noticed it, but when the manager had resumed the conversation after going to the door to close it quite early on he'd asked what was it she had been saying about her friend, only up till that point, Ruth felt sure, she hadn't yet mentioned her cousin or a friend. She and Paul could just as easily have been enquiring about booking a room for a function or anything else that hotels do. A meaningless incident?

The conversion of Mansons' old farm deserved the award it had won.

The raw beams and flagged floor had been kept in the former kitchen, now the bar, with overspill seating in what had been a small dairy and sculleries out in the yard. The two stone barns had been knocked into one and were free for dancing. Historic farm implements and shepherds' crooks decorated the stone walls. Brendan's family, like Brian's, had once been fell farmers and he grew sentimental over the displays.

'Would you like a drink?' Brendan asked.

'Just a fruit juice, please.'

Brendan had the same.

'I never drink and drive,' he said.

They took their drinks and crisps to a table in the corner, where Ruth studied the crowd, looking for Melanie. The only familiar faces she saw, however, had no business being here. The place was eighteen and over only, but Janice Enright's twins walked in, bold as brass, and the barman served them without demur. True, both twins looked older than their fifteen years, but they were local and the man at the bar must surely know their age. Janice, of course, couldn't be aware they were here. They must have told their mother they were going somewhere else.

Should she say something to them? But before Ruth could work out how, Brian had dragged her off to the barn for the disco. Ruth felt out of place and was just wondering if she could escape to the cloakroom when he seemed to come to himself and noticed she was holding back.

'You tired?' he yelled above the heavy beat of the music.

Ruth shook her head, but Brendan took her hand and led her off the floor just the same. Ruth noticed his hands were icy cold.

'Let's have another drink,' he said. 'Kev could probably give you Melanie's address,' he remarked afterwards, the first sign he'd shown of recalling why it was he'd brought Ruth here.

'Who's Kev?'

'The big guy behind the bar.'

'I'll ask him then.'

As Ruth pushed open the door back into the bar, the main door on the far side opened. Janice Enright walked in, then paused. In the shadows behind her was Rudi Leonardson. Ruth hesitated, feeling awkward. Janice glanced round the bar, then leaned back and whispered in her companion's ear. They both turned and retreated out of the bar. In their shadowy corner on the far side, Tim and Emma Enright gave each other a conspiratorial grin. By some miracle their mother hadn't noticed them. What exactly should she do? But before Ruth could take action, the question solved itself. The twins emptied their glasses and slipped away out of the back door.

All the same, Ruth decided she would have a word with Paul. He was good with kids and might have influence with them, or he could alert Janice. The two of them seemed very close. Ruth carried on towards the bar and picked out Kev. It turned out he knew Melanie and promised to pass on

Ruth's message if she happened to come in. He had, however, no idea of her present address.

'She's a girl with a thousand friends,' he remarked.

Brendan was ready to go home when Ruth returned to the disco.

'I'm bushed,' he said.

Ruth wondered again what it was he did that made him so pale and tired.

'I think I know who you are,' he remarked in the van. 'I've been puzzled but you're the girl cousin Brian was engaged to, aren't you? I remember Mum mentioning it. It broke up.'

Ruth nodded.

'What went wrong?'

'We found we weren't suited,' Ruth told him, which was the truth.

Back at Parkways, Brendan tried to hold her back in the van, but Ruth let herself out.

'Don't forget what I said about taking you to see Dr Roberts,' he called after her as she walked away.

'I won't forget.'

It made more sense to ring the doctor up, she thought, but not tonight, it was too late. She could ring Dad, however. He was always late in bed.

She told him Mel had changed her address, and, without mentioning Brendan or the fact that she'd lost her job, said that someone had promised to put her in touch. Dad sounded anxious. Worry was bad for him, so Ruth said nothing about Dr Roberts either.

She'd seen from outside that the light was still on in Paul's room. In the hope of having a word with him about the Enright twins, Ruth dawdled over her milk drink in the lounge but he didn't come down.

In the end Ruth went up to her room. On her way to church yesterday, she'd noticed an empty shop in Market Square, a traditional, stone-built, slate-roofed property, full of character. If Paul agreed, she felt they should look at it. Certainly the place would make a perfect backdrop for a design she had in mind.

6

Just before dawn, Ruth was wakened by insistent tapping at her door. It was Paul, fully dressed, his face white and drawn.

'I've had a call on my mobile,' he explained. 'Aunt Margaret's been taken into hospital with a heart attack.'

'Oh, Paul!'

Ruth reached out and touched his hand. She'd known Margaret Mackay long before she ever met Paul. She was a friendly woman, liked by everyone.

'They don't know without more tests how serious it is.'

'Dad's heart attack three years ago turned out only a mild one,' she consoled him.

'She's in Harleywell Hospital. I'm going straight down. I'll be in touch again when there's more news.'

Ruth pulled open her curtains and

watched him drive away. Then, too sad and troubled to return to sleep, she put in some more work on her project until breakfast time.

Today was their day for learning how to use the new technology. Computer graphics in such a short while was, Ruth felt, beyond her, but, with their tutor's help, she made good use of the highly-sophisticated projectors. By tea-time, she was quite pleased with the results.

For further inspiration, she stopped off for another look at the empty shop in Market Square on her way back to the hotel. As she stood trying to peer in through the dusty windows, a familiar voice hailed her. She recognised it as Janice Enright.

'Have you come to admire my empire?' she asked.

Ruth frowned.

'Where is it?'

She'd forgotten Janice owned a flower kiosk in the town. Now Janice led her to where it was tucked away round the corner just across the square, much too close for comfort if they took on this shop. The rivalry would be intense. Would Paul want that? But Janice was not interested in business today. Her mind was all on Paul and Aunt Margaret.

'He rang me before he set off this morning,' she explained, 'dragged me out of bed in fact. I wanted to go down to the hospital with him, but he refused, to spare me, I think. He knows how I hate hospitals, since my husband died.'

Ruth remained silent.

'Have you ever been in love, Ruth?' Janice asked, unexpectedly.

'I was engaged once,' Ruth told her after a pause.

'But it didn't work out?'

With a deep, sympathetic sigh Janice patted her hand.

'We weren't suited,' Ruth told her in the same words she'd used to Brendan yesterday.

'Trust is the most important thing, I think.'

Ruth nodded. Trust, she was learning, was a complicated matter. Did Janice know about Paul's other life? And the question of Janice's children at the country club also came to mind, but this hardly seemed the time to mention it.

It was quite late in the evening when Paul finally rang to say the news about Aunt Margaret was good. It had been a very minor attack.

'She'll be home in a day or two,' he explained. 'I'm arranging a live-in nurse for her to start with and if all's well, I'll return to Laitheham on Friday, run you to the train in Carlisle on Saturday, then finish my studio calls before returning to Harleywell.'

'Don't forget I can get to Carlisle on the bus,' Ruth pointed out.

'Is everything OK with you?' he asked.

'Fine!' Ruth assured him, deliberately not mentioning that she'd drawn a blank with Dr Roberts' phone number. This wasn't the moment to burden him further with her worries about Mel.

Paul asked her to post some letters he'd left on his desk at the hotel, and when Ruth collected them, her eye fell on his appointments diary, open at today. He'd been booked to have lunch with Janice, she couldn't help noticing. That must be why he'd rung her so promptly to tell her he was going away. For some reason Ruth found herself smiling.

Paul had never mentioned his lunch date with Janice, though. Why should he? Their relationship was nothing to do with her. That was Paul's private life, his own affair.

Having already missed the last collection, Ruth waited a while before going down to the post. The view out over the harbour was magnificent when the street lamps were first alight, as lovely as some of the great bays of the world, Ruth felt. Halfway back up the hill, she paused to admire it. The sea was a pale, uneasy presence beyond the dim outline of the house roofs along the quay, though half-doused nowadays by the fierce security lights in the lorry park. You could see right down into the security pound from here. The lights were so bright Ruth found she could identify two people standing by the surveillance tower, deep in conversation.

What an odd partnership, and what a strange place to encounter them, she thought as she recognised them. But before Ruth could marshal her thoughts to make sense of the scene, she was jolted by a fast car that screeched to a halt right by the kerb, almost knocking her off her feet. It was the girl from Flat A in the Old Vicarage, with her boyfriend at the wheel.

'I wanted to see you,' the girl called through the window. 'I've got some stuff for you. Some things your cousin left when she moved out. I forgot it when you came down before.'

'I see. I'll collect them some time.'

'Make it Thursday evening, after six.'

'Fine,' Ruth agreed.

It wasn't really fine, though. Something was seriously awry if Melanie had started leaving her possessions scattered around. She'd always been neat and tidy to a fault.

The car roared off and Ruth walked on slowly up the hill, completely forgetting what she'd seen in the lorry park.

With Dr Roberts' phone number unobtainable, Ruth decided to go and see him at his address in Carlisle.

Tomorrow afternoon was a free period on the course, when students were allowed to collect information about the area. There was, Ruth knew, a fine archive in the library at Carlisle. She'd go there first, then make a call on Dr Roberts. Her plans left no time for lunch, as it happened, so at the end of the morning she bought a couple of bananas and ate them while waiting for the Carlisle bus.

'Monkey!' the amused comment came as she finished them.

'Brendan!'

He was leaning on the harbour rail, a

mischievous grin all over his face.

'What's wrong with the famous Hall lunch?' he asked.

'We're on a half day today, for local studies.'

'And you're skiving on a bus trip instead?'

'I'm going to Carlisle, to use the library archive. I thought I could call on Dr Roberts at the same time and get Melanie's new address from him.'

Brendan's cheerful grin faded.

'I need to be able to tell Dad Mel's OK, so I want to have a chat with her, and I can't get hold of the doctor's phone number.'

'I'll run you in,' Brendan volunteered. 'I was going into Carlisle anyway and you'll never manage both chores off the bus. There isn't time.'

In Carlisle, Brendan dropped her off near the library with a promise to pick her up there in two hours.

'No,' Ruth said. 'I'll meet you at the carpark.'

She wanted the chance to walk alone

through the familiar streets of the city, her first visit since she'd come three years ago with Brian.

'Please yourself. I'll meet you at the Sands.'

'Fine.'

The Sands carpark, by the leisure centre, was where she and Brian had had their first proper quarrel, after seeing a show. Though only cousins, the two men were as alike as two peas in a pod, even to mannerisms, except emotionally. Brian was hard, ruthless, ambitious. Brendan was soft, a drifter, sweet even. Like his aftershave, the battered old van was fragrant with the scent of lavender. The thought of lavender jangled something unsettling in Ruth's mind, a connection between Brendan and someone else who used lavender, only she couldn't remember who or what it was.

Dr Roberts lived in a cul-de-sac, on a new, upmarket development. Brendan stopped in front of a pair of ornate white gates. It was at the last house in the cul-de-sac. The estate was on the very outskirts of Carlisle, near the motorway. Brendan was right, she'd never have fitted in this visit and the library using the bus.

'It was kind of you to bring me here, Brendan,' Ruth commented as they walked up the tree-lined drive, and without thinking she linked her arm through his.

Brendan's response was flat. Ruth glanced up at him, surprised. His cheerful smile had vanished and the expression in his eyes was sombre, verging on sadness.

'Is everything OK?' Ruth asked. 'You look down.'

'It's just all these trees,' he said. 'They give me the creeps.'

Ruth nodded. It was a sombre place, and empty, not even parked cars as you'd expect at a clinic. Maybe Dr Roberts was so expensive he could grant his patients the privacy of appointments not overlapping.

A receptionist opened the door to

them, took their names, then led them through to a waiting-room that looked more like a drawing-room. The receptionist would, after all, know they weren't patients. These were probably the doctor's private rooms, at the back, overlooking lawns.

Upstairs, music was playing, a string quartet or something of that sort, demanding and austere. Melanie's taste, like her own, was for vocals, especially country style. Some powerful magnetism must have drawn her to this Dr Roberts, so unlike herself. Suddenly the music was switched off. Footsteps sounded on the stairs, then in the corridor. Ruth glanced across at Brendan, whose face had turned very pale.

What was the connection between him and the doctor? He'd said he knew him, and had found the house with no trouble, and now the man's imminent presence clearly troubled him. Had Brendan perhaps come here at one time to remonstrate because Mel had thrown him over for this other man? Ruth felt a pang of remorse. Maybe she'd been wrong to let Brendan bring her here. She knew what it was to feel betrayed.

More likely she was imagining things, Ruth decided when the doctor entered the room. Certainly if he had ever had sharp words with Brendan, he showed no signs of remembering it.

'My secretary says you wish to speak to me,' he said, addressing Ruth, 'but not on a medical matter, I assume.'

He was a tall, strikingly-handsome man in a stern-faced way, grey-haired. His dark eyes betrayed little emotion and his voice was carefully modulated.

'Mr Leonardson at The Highlander in Laitheham gave me your address,' Ruth explained. 'I'm making enquiries about my cousin.'

'Someone I know?'

The inexplicable sarcasm in his voice made her cringe, but Ruth forced herself to stand her ground. She was right to try and find Melanie, who might be in deep distress.

'Melanie Bland is my cousin,' she

explained. 'Mr Leonardson says you may know her present whereabouts. She left her old flat without giving her family a new address.'

Ruth was watching his face and saw his gaze flicker briefly towards Brendan, who glanced away. They had met before, she felt sure of it. The doctor's mouth half formed a denial, but he said nothing aloud. For a while he stood silent, rubbing his chin with his thumb. Then his face softened and he smiled a devastatingly attractive smile.

'Miss Tamworth, confidentiality is fundamental to my work. One gets stuck in a rut and sometimes says no when maybe one should say yes. You're worried about your cousin and it is true I may be able to help. Tell me what you know already and I'll fill in what gaps I can.'

A desire to help was now written all over him, the wish to please, backed up by that smile, a smile to touch a heart of stone, if it was sincere. Ruth told her story.

'You leave me with a guilty conscience,

Miss Tamworth,' the doctor said when she'd finished speaking. 'I myself should have taken the trouble to make sure Melanie was all right after she left me.'

There was a grating harshness in his voice, possibly guilt.

'Unfortunately, she left no address, except what you already know.'

Ruth frowned, disappointed.

'Let me tell you the whole story.'

The doctor sat down facing her.

'I'm a man of the world, I have to say, and live in the real world. I'm married, but my wife and I live separate lives. For financial reasons we have no desire to dissolve our marriage, but we go our own ways. It suits us. Melanie knew all this when we — er — fell in love, if you believe in love at first sight, that is.'

Melanie did believe in love at first sight. It was something they'd discussed, often. Melanie believed that when love came, you'd know it instantly. But what if it was with the wrong man, a married man? That wasn't a life Mel would settle for, Ruth felt sure of it.

'Mr Leonardson told me there had been gossip,' Ruth remarked.

'Of course there was gossip with such a pretty girl.'

'And that's why she was dismissed from her job.'

'Being a hotel — '

'Where did Melanie go, Doctor Roberts, when she lost her job?' Ruth interrupted sharply, irritated by something in his manner.

'Here, of course.'

'You mean Mel's living with you now?'

'I'm afraid not.'

He glanced at Brendan as he spoke, Ruth felt, or maybe he was just avoiding her own eyes. Why did he treat Brendan as a stranger if, as she suspected, they'd met before?

'Where is Melanie then?' Ruth asked. 'Where can I contact her?'

'You should know that better than me, Miss Tamworth. First love doesn't always last through the ups and downs of a shared life, you know. Melanie is very young. There were quarrels and jealousies, misunderstandings. In the end she left me. She told me she was going home.'

'Are you sure that's what she said?'

'She told me she was going home,' he repeated. 'She said it once or twice. Then two weeks ago yesterday, I came back from making some professional visits and found she had packed her things and gone. My secretary, unfortunately, was absent at the time.'

'Well, she never arrived home.'

Where else could Mel go? There was nowhere.

'She left me this note,' the doctor added, pulling a card from his wallet.

The card was clearly characteristic of Melanie, a tiny print of herbs on one side and a simple greeting on the other. A brief message had been scrawled under this.

Sorry it all went wrong. I need to be alone for a while.

The handwriting had an uncharacteristic spikiness, as though Mel had been upset. Ruth handed the card back to the doctor. She'd clearly misjudged him earlier. That he'd kept it was proof that he cared.

'Mel certainly didn't come home,' she repeated with a sigh.

The facts were going to cut Dad to the quick. There was no avoiding the truth. Melanie had taken her unhappiness elsewhere.

'Maybe she's taken refuge with one of her many friends,' Dr Roberts suggested.

Something like a sneer puckered his handsome face, jealousy, probably. He didn't look the type to share what he loved.

'Could you give me the addresses of any of her friends?'

'Don't you think we should respect Melanie's wishes and allow her to be alone if she so wishes, Miss Tamworth?'

This wasn't what she thought, but somehow she agreed. Melanie actually had the right to know her cousin was in the area, and then to make up her own mind what she wanted to do.

84

7

How to contact Melanie, however, wasn't the problem most occupying Ruth's mind as they drove back to Laitheham.

'What's bugging you, Ruth?' Brendan asked her as they consumed the bar meal they'd stopped to have. 'You look like your meal's got no flavour.'

'I can't work out how Dr Roberts knew Paul's aunt has had a heart attack.'

Ruth knew she had told him why she was in Laitheham, and that her companion had been called away because a member of his family was ill. Then, as they were leaving, the doctor had commented how fortunate the lady was to be in Laitheham Hospital, because it was well known for its coronary care. He knew the place, apparently, from having practised there.

'I did mention Laitheham Hospital,' Ruth continued, 'but not that she'd had a heart attack. I'm sure of it.'

Brendan shrugged.

'It's a natural assumption, probably, for a woman of her age.'

'I never mentioned her age, nor even what relationship she is to Paul.'

'He'll be strong on intuition, I reckon. Reading people is as important as reading symptoms in his trade.'

Maybe, only Ruth had the feeling that this was the second incident of the kind this week.

They lingered over the meal, though without pleasure as far as Ruth was concerned. A sulky, truculent mood had had Brendan in its grip since they'd left the doctor's house. It made him uneasy company.

Before they reached Laitheham on the way home he stopped to enjoy the view, so that it was dark by the time he dropped Ruth at Parkways. By that time his bad mood lifted.

'You've got steady nerves,' he remarked

with a smile. 'You never once criticised my driving.'

'You're a good driver,' she replied sincerely.

They both laughed and for a moment the warmth between them was restored. Moodiness, no doubt, was what had ended his relationship with Melanie. She was volatile, but never sulky or withdrawn.

She was quite glad to find his van wasn't there when she called round at the Old Vicarage next day to collect Melanie's things from the girl in the flat. The girl, Patsy, had the items ready for her in an envelope, just one item, as it turned out.

'I found it just under the foot of the bed,' Patsy explained. 'The whole flat had been cleaned before I came, but this must have escaped. Maybe it doesn't belong to your cousin, but I thought it did, because of the initials.'

Ruth reached into the envelope and pulled out an old-fashioned garnet ring with M.A.B. and a date engraved inside the band. As she handled it, Ruth wasn't just worried any more. She felt terrified.

Later, she thought she'd over-reacted. All the same, she extended her booking at Parkways, then rang her dad to explain she was staying on for a few days to work on her project. Afterwards she phoned Paul. He'd rung only that morning to confirm the arrangements he'd made before and sounded surprised to hear her voice.

'What's wrong?' he asked.

'I've just had a change of plan, that's all. I'm staying on in Laitheham for a few days, to work on my project.'

'And?'

'There's something about Melanie, something disturbing.'

'Something new?'

'Yes, and a bit odd. I'll tell you when you come. It's just that I'd like you to bring some letters with you, if you don't mind. All Mel's letters are in a bundle at the bottom of the top drawer of my desk. I want them all. I've told Dad to expect you to call round for them. I said I'd asked you to bring my teenage photo album with you for pictures of Laitheham. The album's with the letters.'

These half-truths were unhappy, but better than worrying Dad.

'Anything else?' Paul asked.

'No, nothing else.'

Next day was the end of Ruth's course, and they finished at lunch-time. Ruth studied the bus timetable and decided she would go to Carlisle, and see Dr Roberts again. She would still be back in time for Paul's return. However, it was a wasted journey. No-one was at home.

Returning down the doctor's drive, she encountered a gardener, trimming the hedge next door.

'The doctor's away,' he told her. 'Left this morning just before lunch, together with his secretary. They had stacks of luggage in the car. He often goes away.'

Ruth thanked him and filled in the wait for the bus home at the library archive, gathering material for her project. She needed that high grade, to prove herself to herself, among other things. Her interest was flagging, overlaid by worry about Melanie. To revive it, she walked up from the bus stop in Laitheham past the shop premises she'd found, then wished she hadn't. Paul had returned early, and his car was parked across the square. She could see him and Janice in deep conversation outside Janice's flower kiosk just round the corner, their heads together, a striking pair.

Janice waved, and Ruth walked towards them feeling in the way. For a moment Janice's face looked taut then it stretched into a welcoming smile.

'The wanderer's returned,' she called out to Ruth.

Paul turned. His face was inscrutable, a cool formality that cut Ruth more than unkind words.

'Did you bring what I mentioned?' she asked him.

'They're in the car.'

A fleeting expression Ruth couldn't read gave his blue eyes a smokey look. Had he been annoyed at her using him as messenger instead of simply asking Dad to post the letters on? Janice linked her arm through Paul's.

'Would you both like to come out and have a meal with me?' she suggested but Paul declined.

'I ought to snatch something to eat quickly and then squeeze in some work,' he explained, 'to prepare for the heap of studio calls still on my list.'

'You're turning into a workaholic, darling.'

'Needs must at the moment, Jan,' he said rather quietly.

Ruth rubbed the cobbles with her toe. On his own Paul would most likely have driven out to Janice's for a meal.

'Have you eaten yet, Ruth?' he asked.

'Not since breakfast,' she admitted. 'I had to skip lunch to catch the Carlisle bus.'

'Carlisle twice in one week! You're getting obsessed with our big city,

Ruth,' Janice commented, with a slanting, sideways glance at Paul.

Ruth sighed. Laitheham hadn't changed. Everyone knew your business and just had to comment.

'It's the best archive library for my project,' she explained.

If she mentioned Dr Roberts it'd soon be all round town!

'I never yet heard of anyone doing library research in company with Brendan Kane,' Janice remarked with a smirk.

'I went on my own today,' Ruth corrected her.

'Already! I hope you two haven't fallen out almost before you've started. I heard it was like two doves up at the country club.'

Paul glanced at her. Ruth bit her lip and made no reply. She didn't like Janice in this mood, and she didn't want to talk about the club, aware she'd still not alerted Janice about the twins. Paul glanced at his watch.

'I'll have to go, Jan. My twenty

minutes parking time is up.'

'See you, darling!' Janice said, giving his arm a squeeze.

Ruth followed Paul towards his car. If Janice hadn't been there she might have pointed out the empty shop she'd found just across the square. As it was, she left it for another time.

Turning to wave before climbing into the car, Ruth surprised an expression of deep resentment on Janice's face, bitter anger, you could almost say. Not, surely, just because Paul, with a mountain of work to do, had opted out of making a round trip of twelve miles to eat at her place. Too late, she realised that good manners demanded that they should have pressed Janice to eat with them, a thank-you for the hospitality they'd received. Paul, clearly, had been too tired and rushed to think of it.

They went to The Highlander, where Paul requested a quiet table. They were placed where they could watch the dusk creeping in over the bay and talk in privacy. Their waiter was the swarthy man Ruth had noticed before.

Over the meal Ruth heard all about Aunt Margaret.

'It's only a very minor attack she had,' Paul concluded. 'The hospital says if she takes it easy for a while and adjusts her lifestyle and diet a bit there's nothing to worry about.'

'Just like Dad three years ago, and avoiding stress, of course.'

'I realise now why you've been so anxious to get news of your cousin. Jo asked me about Melanie when I called round. He seemed quite worried.'

'I'm sure there's something really wrong with her, Paul.'

Ruth paused while the waiter brought their main course.

'I simply can't track down her present address though I've enquired everywhere.'

Ruth told him in detail about her visit to Dr Roberts. Paul asked a few questions, then sat silent for a while.

'Most likely she has moved in with friends,' he said at last.

'Certainly she didn't return home like she told him she would.'

'And what's this something new you mentioned over the phone?'

'This.'

Ruth had taken the garnet ring with her to Carlisle in the hope of showing it to Dr Roberts. She fished it out of her bag and passed it across to Paul.

'Patsy, the girl now in Melanie's flat, found this under the bed.'

Paul turned it over carefully in his fingers.

'M.A.B. Melanie's initials?'

'Melanie Anne Bland, and the date is the date her mother gave it to her. She wears it all the time, never has it off. It belonged to her grandmother and since her own parents divorced, Melanie kept it as a kind of talisman, something that stood for family.'

'Is family something Melanie cares about?'

'Very much.'

'I never thought of her as that kind of girl.'

'She hides it well, but underneath it's top of the list of the things she cares about.'

'Odd, then, that she didn't bother to have this ring repaired. I agree. She certainly couldn't have worn it like this.'

'She'd have turned the place upside down till she found it, Paul. Patsy said it was just under the bed, quite easy to see.'

'You did feel she'd changed since she came to Laitheham,' Paul commented.

'No-one could change that much in just a few months. She'd have kept the ring safe, even if she'd stopped wearing it for some reason.'

Paul said nothing.

'Unless she lost it just as she was leaving the flat and then couldn't come back to hunt for it for some reason.'

'What sort of reason?'

Paul finished eating and nodded to their waiter who was hovering nearby. Ruth waited for him to clear away their plates.

'I don't know, but the ring's not just battered. It's seriously damaged.'

Paul examined it again.

'It isn't split or worn,' Ruth pointed out. 'It's been sheared right through. The broken ends are twisted, as though it was torn apart. That couldn't happen through simple wear and tear.'

The waiter now brought their fruit salad and cream.

'What are you suggesting, Ruth?' Paul asked when they were on their own again.

'It looks as though it was wrenched off Melanie's hand in some kind of struggle, the day she left her flat.'

'You mean it's abduction?'

'You think I'm being fanciful, don't you?'

'Crimes do happen,' he admitted, 'but not usually with no witnesses.'

'Brendan Kane is the only other tenant in the flats. The middle flat is empty, and the day Melanie left, Brendan was away.'

'And where does Dr Roberts come in?'

'I went into Carlisle this afternoon to show him the ring and see what he had to say about it, but he wasn't there.'

'You hadn't made an appointment?'

'You can't. His number's private. You can't ring up.'

Like Melanie — birds of a feather. Paul didn't voice it, but the thought was mirrored in his eyes.

'I brought the letters you wanted by the way,' he remarked after a while. 'There were only five of them. Is that right or did I miss something?'

'No. Mel's not much of a letter-writer.'

No letters, no phone calls — it all added up to a picture of a certain kind of girl, involved in her own life and not caring a toss, but the picture was completely false, Ruth knew, only how to explain that to Paul?

Back at the hotel, they found the lounge empty, so Ruth spread the letters out over the coffee table to read. They were all quite long. When Mel did put pen to paper she usually went to town on it. Paul sat watching her without comment and when Ruth finished reading the letters and glanced up, his face had settled into an uncharacteristic expression, half sad, half amused.

'I missed you in Harleywell,' he remarked, touching her shoulder.

Ruth had missed him, too. She almost said so, but then held back. His words meant nothing. Janice was proof of that.

'I've found what I thought I remembered in the letters,' she said instead.

'Evidence of abduction?'

'Of course not! But listen to this. It says, 'The set-up here seems rather odd. Not that it's anything to do with me.''

'Any more detail?'

'No. But in the same letter she writes, 'I've met someone very very nice. He's taking me to the local country club.''

'The same place you went to with this Brendan Kane?'

'It must be.'

'And Dr Roberts is the someone very, very nice?'

'I'm not sure you'd describe him as nice.'

'So your cousin had another boyfriend then?'

'It does look like it,' Ruth said, her voice full of doubts.

'And you think he abducted her, before or after she'd been staying with Dr Roberts?'

'Don't poke fun at me, Paul. I know it doesn't paint a sensible picture. But if there's nothing odd somewhere, why can't I get an address for Melanie?'

8

Paul felt they should try the country club again, tomorrow. Saturday was no doubt one of their busiest evenings and so more likely to turn up fresh news of Melanie.

Ruth did think she might spend the daylight hours revisiting parts of Laitheham she'd not yet seen, but Paul pressed her to go on a buying trip with him and she agreed. There was so much about the trade she needed to learn. To her surprise Paul had completely vetoed the property in the square she'd found. The decrepit state of the building meant it would cost too much to turn around and it lacked amenities, especially space. Clearly he really was thinking in terms of something more like the Harleywell Craft Centre.

Their route next day took them up the coast to Silloth, then inland, where they stopped for a quick coffee. Paul showed her his itinerary.

'Hexham!' Ruth exclaimed. 'That's almost in Newcastle.'

'But worth it. There's a tapestry weaver there.'

Tapestries! Ruth forced a smile. What she didn't know she'd have to learn, as fast as possible. All this craft work was a far cry from the simple flower shop she and Dad had planned! They went on to visit a small hand-pottery and she found Paul was an expert on the history of the place.

'You're quite the professor,' Ruth teased him.

'Boring, you mean.' Paul grinned. 'I often think it was a blessing for kids when I gave up teaching to run Aunt Margaret's shop for her.'

'Were you a teacher, Paul?'

'Yes. I did the training in Leeds.'

So that's how he came to have friends in Leeds!

'Then I worked in schools for a few years, until Aunt Margaret's health started playing tricks and I had a change of plan.'

'Do you regret it?'

'Not really. I love the craft centre, but I do miss contact with children and youngsters.'

Paul was good with young people. Ruth had seen that at the youth club in Harleywell where she also helped out.

They now drove north, skirting Carlisle, to Brampton, where they stopped for lunch.

'We'll go to Hexham along the Roman Wall,' Paul said.

Somewhere she'd never been with Brian, Ruth thought. She felt her spirits rise. Lanercost Village, with its ruined priory, on their way, was beautiful and she'd not been there since Mum died. She went with Paul to a basket-maker there, then slipped away when it came to the ordering for his shop. Ruth waited for him, leaning on the parapet of the hump-backed bridge. They used to come here as a family. Nothing had changed. The river still tumbled along in fierce pursuit of the same sea that filled Laitheham harbour twice a day.

'What were you thinking?' Paul asked when he joined her on the narrow bridge. 'I was watching your face as I came along the road. First happy, then sad. Then a smile again.'

'I was just remembering Mum, and the way she died.'

Mum had loved this river and wild water in all its forms. Yet in the end the sea had been her enemy.

'You're a person who doesn't forget loss easily, I think.'

'That may be true. I've never thought about it.'

'While I was in Harleywell your father told me that you'd once been engaged.'

'Yes.'

For a moment Ruth felt anxious, reluctant to relive all that with those blue eyes watching her. She couldn't keep Paul at bay with the half-truths she'd given Brendan and Janice. He didn't probe, however, and they returned to the car in companionable silence.

'Next stop, Hexham,' Paul commented.

They drove along the Roman Wall instead of using the main road, and for a reason. Borders history, including the Romans, was the subject of the Hexham weaver's tapestries.

'Modern in style,' Paul explained, 'but based on themes from the past.'

Exactly the line they'd been pushing at Ruth's course. As soon as she saw the tapestries Ruth knew it could work for them. They reflected a sombre era and were all worked in muted shades of black, grey, fawn and cream. They'd make a superb foil for the flowers. For the first time Ruth began to see this merger of studio crafts and flowers through Paul's eyes. It was exciting.

What's more, the weaver treated her as an equal in the trade. Ruth suddenly found she could keep up with the jargon. Somewhere, since leaving the hotel this morning, she'd stopped being a mere spare part.

'Bar snacks aren't enough to sustain

body and soul till tomorrow's break-fast,' Paul declared as they approached Carlisle, and pulled into a quiet restaurant on the outskirts where they had high tea.

As they climbed back into the car Ruth realised, with a sense of shock, that although she had eaten at this restaurant before, with Brian, that she had not once thought of her ex-fiancé until now, and that was only because the name Kane on a passing lorry brought him to mind.

Kane — a name she'd once imagined was going to become her own. Brian Kane . . . Brendan Kane . . . two men so alike and yet so different. They might well meet up with Brendan at the club tonight. Ruth wondered what he and Paul would make of each other.

However, the only personal encounter they had at the club wasn't Brendan at all, it was the Enright twins! Ruth saw them as soon as she walked in, squeezed into the same dark corner as before, just the two of them. She glanced at Paul.

'I'll be with you again in a minute,' he promised, ushering Ruth to a table by the wall, 'but there's a little job I have to do first.'

He walked across to the twins, quiet but determined. Ruth saw their faces change. Not a word of conversation was audible to her, but soon the youngsters stood up, abandoning their drinks. Paul shepherded them out of the main entrance ahead of him. After a while he returned to rejoin Ruth.

'I called a taxi and made sure they were in it. The driver's been given clear instructions to take them home.'

Ruth said nothing. His action spoke volumes about his relationship with the twins' mother.

'Let me tackle the barman straight away,' Paul said, 'before the crowds build up, so that if any friends of Melanie's arrive he can put us in touch.'

Ruth watched him at the bar, hovering between this snack and that, studying all the soft drinks, and talking. When he finally returned with two fruit juices and a couple of mini pizzas he was smiling.

'You've learned something!' Ruth greeted him.

'Kevin says Melanie sometimes used to come here with a fellow called Hugh, a quietish person. He says neither of them has been in for a while.'

'Why ever didn't he tell me that last time?'

'He'd probably forgotten it. Thousands must come here at the height of the season. Your queries may have jolted his memory later.'

Hugh — it wasn't a name Ruth remembered from Mel's letters.

'Kevin thinks he may be able to give us Hugh's phone number if we hang around a bit. There's someone who used to do jobs with him. He's going to give him a tinkle.'

The bar was stifling hot, so they decided to wait outside. Ruth followed Paul through the crowd. She searched for Brendan's face, but didn't see him, to her relief. Brendan stood for things she couldn't share with Paul.

All the seats outdoors were full, so they consumed their snacks propped up against the barn wall. Ruth made conversation by talking about the award-winning décor and what lessons it had for themselves.

'I meant to tell you,' Paul interrupted her. 'Jo's had wind of premises about to come on the market, not yet advertised.'

'Where is it?'

'Down near the harbour.'

Paul gave Ruth details. It sounded perfect, and too far from Janice Enright's kiosk to affect her passing trade.

'You are still keen on the project, aren't you, Ruth?' Paul asked.

'Of course I am.'

Today's brief insight into the world of studio crafts had left her more enthusiastic than before. But it was awkward, this rivalry with Janice. Behind Paul's back, Ruth saw Kevin, the barman, approaching with a slip of paper in his hand. This must be the phone number. Paul hadn't noticed him, his attention distracted by another man tapping him on the shoulder from the other side.

'I think it must be your car that's parked a bit too near the wall, sir,' he was saying. 'There's a van bringing late deliveries and I'm afraid you're in the way.'

Paul went off with him to move his car, so Ruth accepted the slip of paper from Kevin and read it. The number for Hugh Bradshaw was not a local number. Had he moved away, too? And why hadn't Dr Roberts mentioned him? Because Melanie was two-timing and the doctor had not heard of him, Paul would say, but Paul had never met the real Melanie.

'Were you really parked in the way?' Ruth asked him when he returned. 'It's a peculiar time of day to be making deliveries.'

'I suspect there's a supplies crisis.

The driver of the van was someone we know.'

'Who's that?'

'Rudi Leonardson.'

'The manager from The Highlander?'

'The same. I expect they've run short of something here and The Highlander's helping out.'

Brendan had said the manager had his softer side, and his face was kind when he wasn't on the defensive. You could imagine him offering a hand up, even to a competitor. It had always been the Laitheham way of doing things. That, of course, Ruth realised, was why she shouldn't feel nervous about this situation with Janice, especially in view of Janice's relationship with Paul.

Musing on this, Ruth decided, after all, not to tell Paul she'd seen Janice's children at the club last time she came, nor to drop a hint to him that they should perhaps ask Janice to have a meal with them some time. Paul was Dad's business partner. Her rôle was to steer clear of stirring any deep water in his private life. They stayed a little while longer at the club, then Paul said, 'I think we'd better be moving off home.'

Home! Yet in a funny kind of way, Parkways had become more than just a hotel during this past week, especially, somehow, since Paul's absence and return. It was as though Aunt Margaret's illness had changed him, softened him. He no longer scoffed at Ruth's worries about Melanie.

Was it too late to try ringing this Hugh Bradshaw tonight, Ruth wondered, as Paul concentrated on driving along the dark, twisty lanes. She tried to read her watch by the faint light from the dashboard. She was just holding it up close to her face to see it better, when she was blinded by brilliant headlights right in her eyes as they rounded yet another sharp bend.

Paul braked hard. The car stayed steady for a moment then went into a spin. Paul brought it under control again, but they slithered off the road and bumped across a rutted verge before plunging nose first into a ditch. Their seatbelts held them, but Ruth felt bruised all over. In the turmoil, she'd dropped her bag. She started groping on the floor of the car for it.

'Leave that,' Paul commanded, 'and get out, in case there's a fire.'

He struggled out of his own door, then came round and opened Ruth's door, wedged firm against a bush.

'That bush may have saved our lives,' he commented.

It had slowed their progress so that the car had not plunged right down into the depths of the ditch.

'It was you who saved our lives, Paul,' Ruth commented, standing close to him in the cold air. 'Your driving was excellent.'

'I did an advanced driving course. It seemed the thing to do when I spend so much time on the road.'

Ruth was shivering with shock, so Paul took off his jacket and slipped it round her shoulders.

'Though it's better to stay clear of accidents than to have to cope with them afterwards!' he added.

How calm he sounded. Ruth stilled her shaking hands and pulled his jacket tight against the cold wind. Cautiously Paul opened the boot and pulled out a torch. The car was damaged, of course. He fished his mobile out of his jacket pocket.

'I'd better ring the police,' he said.

They arrived quickly, and having listened to Paul's account, and Ruth's, they took a number of measurements.

'There's been a spate of these incidents recently,' one officer commented. 'Probably the same careless driver all the time, someone who needs a word in their ear about dipping lights on bends.'

'This oil on the road was the main culprit,' his colleague pointed out.

They went off together to examine it.

'Did you see anything of the car, sir?' they asked Paul when they returned but he hadn't, nor had Ruth.

'Mind you, I thought it was parked,' Paul said.

'Yes,' Ruth agreed. 'I'm sure I saw it pull away just as we were skidding out of control.'

'In a hurry to escape before they found themselves involved with the law, I imagine, miss.'

'It was a ridiculous place to park a car.'

'Courting couples usually pull off in the lay-by down the road,' Ruth commented, 'and it's not a likely time of day for farmers to be tending stock.'

Paul laughed.

'Probably some tourist had stopped to admire the distant gleam of Laitheham Bay under the stars.'

Ruth forced a laugh as well. There was just this one short stretch of road where you could see the bay from up here, a favourite haunt of those with romance in their hearts. She'd been here with Brian and Paul clearly knew it.

Back at the hotel Paul rang the

late-night number of the local garage about his car, then insisted they had hot drinks and biscuits in the lounge. Ruth still felt cold and shivery. Paul put his arm round her. Exhausted, she leaned on him, taking strength from his strength.

9

Paul's arm round her was the first thing Ruth remembered when she woke next morning, the smooth softness of his shirt, the hint of cologne in his aftershave. Then the rest came back, the accident.

Today was a glorious day, a Sunday, a day she might never have seen except for Paul's superb driving. His hands on the wheel and his arm round her shoulders — how reassuring they were. Yet when he pressed her later to go with him on his trip up into the Scottish Borders, Ruth declined.

'Either it's the hire car or you don't trust my driving any more.'

Ruth smiled.

'You know I trust you but you're visiting friends, not just a business trip. You'll be better on your own.'

'Any friends of mine will be welcome at their house, Ruth.'

Paul shot her a sharp, enigmatic glance. For a moment Ruth wavered, then she shook her head. This was his private life. Wiser not to trespass.

'In any case,' she pointed out, 'I need more Laitheham material for my course project and today's perfect for photography.'

One picture she wanted was of the congregation coming out of church, which could only be done today. For her theme of Laitheham Then and Now it would pair well with an old photograph Dad happened to have of the Blessing of the Fishing Fleet in the nineteenth century.

After church, Ruth returned to the hotel to phone Hugh Bradshaw's number. Last night she'd stuffed the slip of paper in her drawer. As she pulled it out she dislodged the envelope with Melanie's ring in it. It slipped out. Ruth shivered. Yesterday had been a forward-looking day, softening her fears. Then the accident had driven everything else right out of her mind. But somewhere behind the mystery of Melanie's disappearance from Laitheham, violence was lurking, she was sure of it.

A quiet person, the barman had described Hugh Bradshaw, but brutality didn't always partner a loud voice. It was essential to contact Melanie herself, to hear from her own lips that everything was OK.

Ruth wished she'd rung up while Paul was still on hand to offer support, in fact it wasn't needed, at least not yet. At her first try the number was engaged. Then she kept getting no reply. In the end Ruth decided it best to leave it until later in the day and set out with the camera.

First she went past the house where she'd lived as a child, traditional slate and brick. The floppy white rose was in full bloom. Ruth took a few photos. Then she headed for the harbour, striving to see things from a visitor's point of view. Tucked away in a corner just off the quay she found a new restaurant, open only at weekends. She bought some postcards for friends at home, and studied some local brochures.

Some of the postcards gave Ruth ideas for more photos. On her way out in search of them she bumped into the dark-haired waiter from The Highlander. He'd been studying the menu on the wall. Ruth stopped to read it, too. The restaurant offered a special Sunday evening menu which looked good. She might suggest it to Paul for tonight.

She tried Hugh Bradshaw's number again from a call-box on the harbour, but once again, no-one answered. Across the road was the back entrance to the lorry park, the entrance she and Melanie had used on their way home from school, stopping off to see if Dad was back.

Laitheham Then and Now — Dad had some pictures of his three wagons on the hard-standing. She could take a few shots of the new development to go with them. Though no doubt it brought much-needed money to the town, the place was now an eyesore, especially the secure compound with its massive lamps. Ruth did her utmost to find views that made the best of it.

Maybe some of the drivers would patronise their new shop. Several of the parked lorries were foreigners, the new Laithcham. Ruth moved closer in for a shot of them. Being early afternoon on a Sunday the yard was sluggish and no-one seemed to mind her standing right by the loading-bay. It was exciting in its way, these huge wagons from all over Britain and Europe, like the foreign cargo boats they used to see in the harbour years ago.

Someone appeared on the roof of the central office and went up into the surveillance tower, a tall figure wearing a navy donkey-jacket and a woolly hat. The look-out, Ruth thought with a smile, remembering the actual look-out they'd still had in the harbour when she was a child.

This man had a familiar air, but she

couldn't identify him, not with that thick, knitted hat pulled right down over his ears. At least it wasn't the ubiquitous Rudi Leonardson! The manager was a much shorter man.

Ruth took a few more photos and then rang Hugh Bradshaw's number again. This time she had success.

Delayed by the week-end holiday traffic, Paul arrived back late that evening. Ruth half wondered if he might have invited Janice to eat with them, but he hadn't, so she recommended the restaurant she'd found earlier. Over their meal, Paul told her at length about the friends he'd visited, who also happened to run a craft studio. Ruth wondered why he was going into so much detail about this one visit until he mentioned that they were related to Janice Enright. Paul was, perhaps, trying to tell her something in an oblique way. It wasn't until they reached the coffee that he asked after her phone call to Hugh Bradshaw.

'Did it work out OK?' he asked.

'Sort of.'

'What does that mean?'

'It turned out to be a hotel number and they said Hugh Bradshaw used to work for them but had moved on.'

'Did they tell you where to?'

'They gave me a phone number, in Germany! A place called Travemuende. They said he'd gone to work there as a temp. I rang it straight away.'

'And you spoke to him?'

'I got hotel reception first, but when I asked for Hugh Bradshaw, they put me through.'

'Do you speak German?'

'No, but as soon as the receptionist realised I was English she switched to very good English.'

'What did Hugh Bradshaw say about Melanie?'

'He told me Mel's at the hotel with him. He has rooms there.'

'And you spoke to her?'

'No. He said she was out when I rang.'

'Did he say how long Melanie had

been with him in Germany?'

Paul sounded distracted.

'A couple of weeks or so, he said. He mentioned she'd had an unhappy relationship break-up and gone out there for a rest, to get over it, before preparing for her college course.'

'That sounds about square with everything else we've heard.'

'Yes, though he said nothing about losing her job.'

Ruth wished Paul sounded less distracted, almost bored.

'The last thing is, you see — '

'Am I imagining things, Ruth,' Paul interrupted her, 'or is that fellow watching us?'

So that's what's on his mind! Ruth glanced round and saw the dark-haired waiter from The Highlander at a table in the far corner, just finishing his meal. He met Ruth's eyes, smiled, then stood up and came across.

'Excuse the interruption,' he said, 'but I heard you the other day make an enquiry at The Highlander about Miss

Melanie Bland.'

'Yes?'

Paul's tone was stiff and unwelcoming.

'For news of her, best to go to her friend at Silloth.'

'What friend?' Ruth asked.

'Mr Hugh Bradshaw.'

Ruth glanced at Paul.

'I give you the address of his family, madam,' the waiter continued, pulling a card from his pocket.

'We don't need that now,' Paul said. 'We've been in touch with him by phone.'

'At his family?'

'No, in Germany.'

The waiter shook his head.

'Much better to visit his family,' he insisted, and finished writing the address on the card, which he handed to Ruth.

Then he paid his bill and left the restaurant ahead of them. He was still lurking in the carpark when they emerged. He came across and went through the same speech all over again, before hurrying away towards the harbour. Turning, she caught sight of Rudi Leonardson climbing out of his car, parked along the road. The manager strode into the restaurant carpark with a grim look on his face. Catching sight of them, he waved, though without smiling.

'I wonder what he's doing here,' Paul remarked.

'Perhaps this restaurant is under the same management as The Highlander. That would explain why the waiter was eating here instead of on his own patch.'

'You don't really want to do what that waiter suggested, do you, Ruth?' Paul asked as they drove up through town.

Ruth hesitated.

'Probably not,' she agreed after a pause.

'What's to be gained by going to Silloth?'

'Nothing really,' she replied.

They'd reached the hotel carpark. Paul turned off the engine and turned to face her.

'What's wrong?' he asked. 'You're

really upset about something. I can hear it in your voice.'

Ruth bit back the tears she'd been struggling with all evening.

'It seems so odd, somehow, Mel running off to Germany when she's unhappy, instead of coming home.'

'Some people really can only share their deepest feelings with a tiny handful of people they're closest to, Ruth.'

'But we are the people she's closest to. We're her family.'

'Yes, but not her closest family. She's only your cousin, isn't she?'

'But we're more like sisters. Mel's mother was Mum's sister and Mum and Dad had her come and live with us after her parents divorced, because she couldn't get on with either of her new step-parents. She's lived with us since she was eleven. Mel loves her parents, but Dad is very special, too.'

'I didn't realise that,' Paul said thoughtfully. 'My folks divorced. Though Dad never remarried, Mum did. I stayed with Dad, but all the same Aunt Margaret was a haven during the unsettled times. I owe a lot to her.'

'You'd never risk hurting her, would you?'

'No.'

'And Mel wouldn't risk hurting Dad.'

They sat on silently for a few moments. Paul put his arm round Ruth, and she realised that tears were trickling down her cheeks.

'I don't know what I can tell Dad,' she said.

'What information did you actually get from Hugh Bradshaw?'

'Not much really, and he sounded sort of odd.'

'Odd?'

'Strained, as if he was reading a speech, and his voice wasn't at all what I was expecting. In her letter Mel said that someone nice she'd met had a gorgeous Cumbrian accent. This person spoke like someone from a public school.'

'Some people do have two voices,' he pointed out.

His easy acceptance of the fact was like a whip across Ruth's face. Did he have two sides, too?

'Mind you,' Paul added, 'to my eye there's beginning to be just too many odd items in all this with Melanie. First no-one knows where she is. Then the damage to her ring, now this with Hugh Bradshaw's accent.'

'And that waiter's insisting we should visit Hugh Bradshaw's family.'

'They're all little things, only together they look peculiar.'

'I did think I might ring back later to see if I could talk to Mel in person,' Ruth admitted, 'just to be sure.'

'Right, but what about me making the actual call with you standing by my side, so that it's a different voice calling?'

'All right, let's do that.'

Paul's train of thought was all too obvious — and not a happy one.

10

Paul tried the German number twice that evening and then next day, both before and after breakfast, but got no reply.

'They must all be either busy or out,' Ruth remarked after the fourth attempt.

'I don't believe this place is a hotel at all. However small, without someone to man the phone they'd have no bookings.'

'But the woman I talked to, and Hugh Bradshaw — '

'If it was Hugh Bradshaw.'

'What are you saying, Paul?'

At last he was voicing her own thoughts, shadowy fears she kept trying to chase away.

'Something or nothing. I scarcely know myself.'

'Let's go and see Hugh Bradshaw's family in Silloth, Paul, like that waiter suggested. We could go this evening.'

'No, that's another day wasted. Let's go now.'

'But what about your business calls?'

'This is more important.'

Ruth loved Silloth. Even her worries about Melanie couldn't cloud the happy memories of the homely seaside resort. Many of those memories included Melanie. They used to spend hours playing hide-and-seek or cryptic messages in the sand dunes beyond the harbour.

The day was bright and sunny. Here, the Solway Firth was narrower than at Laitheham and the Scottish hills were crystal clear, blue and sparkling in the rain-washed distance.

That feeling of closeness with Paul was there again as, without thinking what she did, Ruth allowed him to grasp her hand in his as they set out along the promenade towards the harbour and the address the waiter had given them. The neat, red-brick terrace house they came to bolstered her hopes. It seemed so homely and ordinary.

A young woman with a baby in her arms opened the door to them and Ruth's heart sank. Was Hugh another married man? Was that why the waiter had pushed them to come here? Ruth felt suddenly cold, yet she still couldn't believe her cousin had changed that much.

'Does Mr Hugh Bradshaw live here?' Paul asked.

The young woman's eyes opened wide and she pulled the door closed behind her.

'Hugh's not had an accident?' she whispered.

'Not so far as we know. It's just that a friend of ours has moved without leaving an address, and someone told us — '

'You'd better come in,' the woman said. 'I'm Hugh's sister, Eve. You need to talk to Mam.'

She spoke with a strong Cumbrian accent.

'These people are friends of our Hugh, Mam,' she explained as she ushered them into a tidy front parlour where a brisk fire burned in the grate.

It wasn't exactly true, but Ruth didn't disillusion her. The older woman's face had brightened like a cloud lifting at the information.

'If you've any news of the lad I'll be glad to hear it,' she said. 'He's not rung home for weeks or been through to see us like he usually does.'

She had dark circles under her eyes, as though she lacked sleep.

'We're not allowed to ring him at that hotel,' Eve explained, 'and I didn't like to ask my husband to run us down there one evening, just in case.'

Their eyes met, and Ruth saw that Eve had fought, and lost, the same battle she was fighting with herself over Melanie — keeping faith, believing against the evidence.

'I'm afraid we haven't brought any news about Hugh,' she apologised. 'We were hoping you'd be able to tell us where he is now.'

'He's at The Highlander till October,'

Mrs Bradshaw told them. 'Then he's moving to one of those big London hotels.'

'What job does he do, Mrs Bradshaw?' Paul asked.

'He's a chef, a good one, one of the best.'

'He's hoping to set up his own restaurant,' Eve added.

'You've not heard him mention going to work in Germany for a while?' Paul asked. 'Or maybe being seconded there, either from The Highlander, or from the chain it belongs to?'

Did the hotel belong to a chain? Ruth hadn't thought of that. It could explain how Hugh had moved on to one hotel and then another, moves his family clearly knew nothing about. Rudi Leonardson was German, or perhaps Austrian.

'Germany?' Mrs Bradshaw said and looked puzzled. 'The lad's not mentioned anything.'

'But then we haven't heard from him, you see,' Eve added.

Mysterious silences; moves without explanation; all out of character, just like Melanie. Ruth shivered in spite of the bright fire.

'Maybe he's taken a holiday,' Eve suggested.

'He's not owed any holiday from this job, lass. Though he's a good chef he's only a fill-in there, you know.'

'He might have twisted their arm to give him a few days break with his girlfriend, Mam. He's a canny talker, our Hugh.'

'And with a Cumbrian accent?' Paul interposed.

'Cut it with a knife!' Eve laughed.

'What's this girlfriend's name?' Ruth asked.

'Melanie. Unusual, and such a pretty name.'

'She's a pretty lass as well, isn't she, Mam?'

'You mean you've met her? Melanie's my friend's name, the friend I'm looking for. She's my cousin, actually.'

'We've not actually met her,' Mrs

Bradshaw explained, 'but Hugh sent us some photos of the pair of them. We thought it looked serious.'

'Do you still have the photos?' Paul pressed.

'Of course I have!'

Mrs Bradshaw pulled them out of the sideboard drawer. Ruth glanced at Paul and nodded. The photos were definitely of Melanie. Ruth opened her mouth to say so, but Paul silenced her.

'That's certainly our friend, Mrs Bradshaw,' he said, 'so we know now that we can find her through your Hugh.'

He stood up ready to depart.

'At The Highlander in Laitheham,' Eve reminded them.

'And when you see him, tell him his mam wouldn't mind a call sometime,' Mrs Bradshaw added with a strained smile as they left.

'Was that right, Paul, misleading them, not telling them what we know?' Ruth asked as they strolled back to where they'd left the car.

'It's not always easy to know what to do for the best.' Paul sighed. 'I thought it might be better to have more information first.'

'Not go stirring things.'

Ruth echoed his sigh. It sounded as though Melanie must have been involved with Hugh at the same time as she was still with Dr Roberts. Mel never used to be a girl to have two strings to her bow, but the difference was one Paul might not understand.

'What do you think I ought to do now about Melanie, Paul?' Ruth asked. 'What can I do?'

'We need to go further with this hotel in Germany.'

'How?'

'I have a friend in Hamburg. He may be able to help. I'll contact him.'

Back in Laitheham they noticed a police car parked outside The Highlander as they passed, but they kept on to their own hotel, where Paul rang his friend in Hamburg while Ruth sifted fruitlessly through Melanie's letters for any more information about Hugh Bradshaw. Mel did say that the someone very, very nice worked at The Highlander, but Ruth had noticed that before.

'Frank Martin in Hamburg says Travemuende's only about an hour's drive from him,' Paul told her when he'd finished on the phone. 'He's going to visit this Hotel Graulhof and ask a few questions.'

'He may actually be able to talk to Melanie.'

'I asked him to see her if he possibly could. I told him how worried we were.'

Well, Paul had come right round to her point of view. He was now a friend she could lean on.

'If this draws a blank, we ought to consider going to the police, I think,' he added.

'When will your friend ring back?'

'Late evening. No earlier. He has appointments this afternoon.'

More time to kill, more anxious, wasted hours Ruth thought and looked round for some way to use the time profitably.

'We could see if we can find these shop premises on the harbour that Dad's got wind of,' she suggested.

It would serve to occupy their minds.

They soon found the only possible location, a spacious, modern unit in one of the former warehouses, empty, but with no agents' signs up yet. As far as they could tell from outside there was good selling space on two floors, storage at the back and in a cellar, which would be perfect for flowers. Apart from decorating and refitting, no work was needed.

'Dad'll like that it's so near where he used to keep his wagons,' Ruth commented.

'Shall we ring him and tell him we like the look of it?'

Ruth hesitated.

'No, wait till there's firm news of Melanie.'

'We must celebrate, though.'

Ruth smiled.

'Shouldn't we wait till we've succeeded first?'

'This is success, our feet on the first rung of the ladder.'

Ruth laughed at his enthusiasm.

'Let's have that cream tea we promised ourselves when we arrived,' Paul suggested. 'They do a good one at the golf club restaurant, I believe.'

Their way to the golf club took them past Parkways. In their absence, the garage had returned Paul's car, repaired, and left a note to say they'd collect the hire car later on. They were still reading the note when Mrs Saunders came running down the hotel steps.

'What a piece of luck!' she exclaimed. 'There's a phone call for you, Mr Mackay. I saw you through the window and asked them to hold on.'

Frank Martin already? Sensing trouble, Ruth followed Paul, who hurried ahead to take the call. He was just setting down the receiver as she arrived.

'Whatever is it, Paul?'

'It's Aunt Margaret. She's had

140

another heart attack, a bad one this time. That was the hospital.'

'I'll help you collect your things.'

Paul reached out and clasped her hand.

'Shall I come with you?' Ruth asked. 'I'm not sure you ought to drive.'

'No. You stay here and wait for Frank Martin's call. I'll be OK. It's just the shock. The doctors told me she was fine. I would never have come back here to Laitheham otherwise. I'd have stayed on in Harleywell with her.'

'She'll know that, Paul.'

No-one could doubt his devotion to his family.

Paul had hardly driven away and Ruth had gone to her room when Mrs Saunders came up and knocked at Ruth's door.

'There's a policeman to talk to you, Miss Tamworth,' she said with a worried frown. 'He's in the office.'

Police? Had Paul had another accident? She should never have let him drive down to Harleywell alone. Ruth ran down to the office with her hands trembling. It was the same officer who'd taken the lead when Paul called the police after he'd run off the road up on the fell.

'Just routine, Miss Tamworth,' he assured her straight away, 'but I believe you were with Mr Brendan Kane in Carlisle on Wednesday afternoon.'

'That's right.'

'Well, I just need to check he was OK when he left you, Miss Tamworth.'

'Yes. He seemed fine to me.'

'You're probably the last person to see him alive, you see. He crashed his car on the track across the road here down into Laitheham. It's a very dangerous stretch of road, unmade and twisty, and steep as a cliff.'

'That's why Brendan uses it. He likes the challenge. He drove that old rust heap of a van partly for the fun of coaxing it along roads other drivers couldn't manage.'

Brendan dead! She'd known him only a few days, but the shock of his death was piercing.

'You wouldn't say he seemed ill or anything, miss? He hasn't been drinking, nothing of that sort?'

'He always stuck to fruit juice when he was driving, and I don't believe he was ill.'

Brendan had seemed in a funny mood, Ruth remembered, but it no way affected his driving. She'd noticed that at the time.

'Right, thank you, Miss Tamworth. That's what we thought. There are a few more questions as well, I'm afraid, just routine.'

Ruth asked a few questions of her own as well and learned that Brendan had apparently swerved off the track on a sharp bend and plunged into a pit left by the quarry there years ago. No-one used the track much nowadays and his car had remained unnoticed till early this morning, when one of the golf-course workers had gone that way.

Ruth had vowed to walk that track, she remembered, because it was a walk she'd never tried before. If she'd kept her vow Brendan would have been found earlier, though not in time to save his life. The officer said he almost certainly died instantly on impact with the quarry wall.

Alone in her room Ruth shed tears for him. Though she'd known him only a few days he'd winkled his way into her affections, with his desire to help and his knack of reaching out one minute then quickly disappearing into his shell again, more moody than anyone she'd ever known.

Like, yet unlike, his cousin, Brian, Brendan had acted as a catalyst and helped her look again at the intense infatuation she'd had for Brian and weigh up how it ended. It had been infatuation, not love. Months ago Melanie had warned her she was still carrying a torch for Brian, a false light, she'd called it. Ruth had scoffed at the idea. Melanie had been right, though, and in some unfathomable way, Brendan had helped her to put that torch down.

Genuine sorrow and distress for his sudden, shocking death racked Ruth for a while. But this grief was nothing compared with the pain that had stabbed through her when for a moment she'd believed the police officer had come with news that Paul had been in a second crash, a fleeting, bitter anguish that had caught her by surprise.

Brendan, no doubt, was why that police car had been parked outside The Highlander earlier, since he lived in one of the hotel's flats, and worked for them. Jolted into awareness by the shock of his death, Ruth suddenly remembered something she'd forgotten, seeing Brendan and Rudi in close conversation under the bright lights of the lorry park.

An odd combination, she'd thought at the time, but had dismissed it. Now, however, she made sense of it. The hotel must have employed Brendan to ferry supplies from delivery wagons, a far cry from the grandiose assignments he'd hinted at! To ease her feelings, Ruth decided to take a walk while waiting for the call from Frank Martin in Hamburg to come through. Late evening Paul had said, hours away. As she crossed the foyer Mrs Saunders called out to her.

'There's a letter in your pigeon-hole, Miss Tamworth, in case you'd not noticed. It came in the post this morning.'

Ruth wasn't expecting a letter. She pulled out the plain white envelope and opened it. A single white sheet contained just a few words, typed: YOUR FRIEND IS IN DANGER. DO NOT GIVE UP YOUR SEARCH. It wasn't signed. Ruth glanced at the envelope again. It was clearly meant for her, though her surname had been spelled Tamword instead of Tamworth. The postmark was local.

Whoever could have sent it? Not Brendan, certainly. Deep in thought, she didn't hear Janice Enright enter the foyer and walk up to her. She was right at her shoulder and had read the note before Ruth could fold it up out of the way. Janice's eyebrows rose.

'Have you had this kind of thing before?' she asked.

'It must be a crank, someone who knows I'm trying to contact Mel and gets a kick out of alarming people.'

Dozens of people must have heard her or Paul making enquiries at the country club and on her first visit there she'd given the barman her name and told him she was staying at Parkways, in the hope that he'd pass on the information to Melanie.

'Haven't you linked up with your cousin yet?' Janice enquired.

Paul hadn't been keeping her in the picture then. Ruth started to tell her about Hugh Bradshaw and the hotel in Germany, but Mrs Saunders came across from the office and interrupted them.

'If you've brought the fresh flowers I'll help you with them, Janice,' she said.

'I do all the house plants and flower arrangements here,' Janice pointed out to Ruth.

Ruth glanced past her at the heap of cartons stacked by the reception desk. Floristry was her own skill, of course, one she'd received awards for through the chain that owned the flower shop in Harleywell.

'I'll help you with the flowers, Janice,' she volunteered.

'If you want to.'

Her tone was unwelcoming, but Ruth ignored it. Contact with flowers was soothing and restful, something she needed now.

'Have you heard about Brendan?' Ruth asked after a while.

'What's the fool been up to this time?' Janice sneered.

Ruth wished she'd said nothing.

'He's dead,' she explained. 'The police told me a little while ago. I was the last person to see him alive, apparently.'

'Brendan Kane dead?' Mrs Saunders,

who had overheard, asked. 'What happened?'

'He crashed his car on that quarry track across the road.'

'Crashed his car? That's terrible!'

Mrs Saunders and Janice spoke in unison. But Mrs Saunders seemed simply shocked, Ruth noticed, while Janice looked almost scared and her hands started shaking.

'Where's Paul?' she asked tensely, as though desperate to talk of something else.

'Hasn't he rung you? His aunt's had another heart attack, a serious one this time.'

Janice banged down the box of pot plants she was unpacking. Her hands were still shaky, the first time Ruth had seen her less than in total control.

'He never rang me,' she remarked.

'He only heard a couple of hours ago,' Ruth apologised for him. 'Maybe he phoned and you were out.'

'I'm not tied to pigeon-post. I use a mobile.'

'He'll have had his foot down hard all the way to the hospital, I imagine. I expect he'll ring when there's definite news.'

'I expect he will.'

Janice made a visible effort to master her mood, flipping back her curls behind her ears.

'We're making plans for a party next month for the twins' sixteenth birthday.'

Strange, Ruth felt, that Janice could think of parties at a time like this, or perhaps not. This was a family party, a message, a token, perhaps a discreet, unspoken announcement to the world for Paul and Janice, too. Love didn't have to blossom into wedding bells. They were both people of the world.

For the first time ever, Ruth suddenly found no comfort in her work. The yellow roses Janice had brought for the reception desk were perfect, fragrant and intense, but she had to force herself to concentrate on trimming them.

'You've a real gift for flower work,'

Janice commented.

Generous words, but her face was sour.

'Where do you go now?' Ruth asked, helping her reload the empty cartons and buckets in her van.

'Down to The Highlander. Rudi Leonardson knows how to appreciate me,' she said, obviously still riled by Paul overlooking her.

Ruth watched her drive off down the hill. Hadn't Janice once told her she didn't do the flowers at The Highlander? She must have won the contract recently, through her friendship with Rudi Leonardson, perhaps. His name again. Paul was right — first Brendan, now Janice. Wherever you turned, you found Rudi Leonardson.

11

Instead of setting off for the walk she promised herself, Ruth decided to ring Dad with the news about Margaret Mackay, since the two of them were friendly with one another. She found him already in low spirits.

'I've had a letter from Melanie,' he told Ruth after she'd given him her news.

A letter! Ruth hid her agitation.

'She's in Germany, lass. Gone off for a bit of a rest, she says, with a friend.'

'Someone here told me the same thing, Dad.'

It was important to play it down and not encourage him to feel upset, but it was difficult.

'You'd think the lass'd rather come home if she needs a bit of a rest,' he went on.

'You know Mel, Dad. Anything new

and she's off after it.'

Dad fiddled with the phone for a moment without speaking.

'Does Mel give any news in her letter, Dad? Tell us where she's staying or anything?'

'She says she's at a place called Travemuende, in a hotel. She says it's on the Baltic and her friend works there.'

At least that tallied with what they'd been told. Should she inform Dad about Paul's friend in Hamburg who was looking into things? No, better not. It might worry him.

'Does Mel tell us when she's coming back, Dad?' Ruth asked instead.

'No, but she can't stay very long. There's her job to consider.'

Too late, Ruth wished she'd told Dad about Melanie losing her job when she'd first heard the news.

'I think there may be difficulties with her job at The Highlander,' she ventured, paving the way.

But Dad didn't seem to hear.

'She enclosed a lock of her hair in her letter, Ruthie,' he continued with his own news.

'A lock of her hair?'

'Yes. A long length, as though she'd cut it off with a knife, it was so ragged.'

'Does Mel say why she sent it?' Ruth asked, struggling to sound calm.

'No, lass. I couldn't make it out at all.'

'Maybe she'd had her hair cut and this is a memento.'

This idea satisfied Dad, and they talked for a while about the swimming pool fund and other things. Ruth rang off leaving him in a more cheerful frame of mind. She set down the receiver with relief. Play-acting wasn't something she liked, but she hid her fears. Sending a lock of her hair in a letter without any explanation was completely out of character for Mel.

So what did it mean? What exactly was going on?

Ruth was still trying to work this out when Frank Martin rang from Hamburg, earlier than she'd expected. He'd been to the Hotel Graulhof in Travemuende and found the place shut up and out of use, awaiting refurbishment.

'Tell Paul from me I think he ought to consider contacting the police,' he said before he hung up.

Ruth went downstairs and ordered a coffee and a snack in the lounge. All her earlier trembliness had gone and her brain was working overtime. Frank Martin was right. She must contact the police. But how to make the message into sense? How to convince strangers that all these little incidents with Mel were completely out of character, and that's what made it so certain something was wrong somewhere?

How could she convince them Mel had never been a two-timer, so something there was false, that she'd always been very caring towards her family, so her long silence had been a message in itself. What had happened to her ring had a story to tell, too, and she would never have sent Dad a lock of her hair without some message to explain why.

The word, messages, Ruth realised after a while kept flicking into her mind, and images of games they used to play as children — Cryptic Messages, the game where you left a clue and the others had to work out what it meant before a count of fifty or something. Could all these little incidents be cryptic messages?

If so, what did they mean? Why was Mel sending them?

Paul had laughed at her picture of Mel's violent abduction from her flat, yet such things did happen. People were held against their will. Hugh Bradshaw's family seemed nice, but what about the man himself? Had Melanie dragged off her own precious ring, deliberately damaged it, and thrust it in a corner under her bed, in the hope that someone would find it and return it to her home address, to her family, people who knew her and would understand how to read the clue?

Even Paul wasn't really laughing at such notions any more, she knew. If

Frank Martin drew a blank, he'd said, they must go to the police. So she must do it now, not by phone, though. She needed to talk to an officer in person and make sure he wrote things down in full understanding of the facts. Too much valuable time had already been lost.

It was over an hour now since Frank Martin had called.

After leaving a message for Paul in case he rang, Ruth ran up to her room for a warm sweater.

Ruth's room was on an upper, inner corridor. The corridor had no windows, lit only by electric light. The lights, she found, had failed. Nothing happened when she pressed the switch. Ruth waited for a moment for the emergency lighting to come on. When it didn't she groped her way along the dark corridor towards her door, the third on the right, exactly at the top of a short flight of steep stairs at the far end, leading to the hotel service area. She ought to alert someone on her way out that the lights weren't working.

Just before she reached her door, she thought she heard someone coming towards her in the darkness.

'Be careful!' Ruth called out.

Immediately, she was completely blinded by a brilliant flash of light, just for a second, as though the lights had come on then gone out again. Ruth faltered under the shock, and found herself entangled in something left in the middle of the corridor. Battling to keep her balance, she stumbled down the stairs, dragging the heavy object with her. She managed to grab a banister to save her fall, and the object continued alone, down the stairs.

Again Ruth thought she heard someone and called out a warning. Again, no-one replied, and certainly no-one else had a room up on this corridor. Bruised and shaky, she felt her way back to her room and fetched her torch. The object she'd fallen over was a vacuum cleaner with its hose attached. Rather than make trouble for the cleaner who'd left it in such an unsuitable place Ruth stacked it away in a corner and contented herself with reporting the failed lights and emergency back-up at Reception.

'Mrs Saunders'll be ever so upset,' Ellie said who was on duty. 'The emergency lights should never fail.'

'There was no harm done,' Ruth assured her.

By sheer luck, as an older guest might have sustained serious injuries, Ellie pointed out.

As she turned away from the desk, Ruth noticed another letter in her pigeon-hole. Like the previous letter it was addressed to Miss Tamword instead of Tamworth, but this one had been delivered by hand. Ruth asked Ellie if she'd seen who brought it, but she hadn't.

'I was away getting my coffee for half an hour,' she explained, 'and there's no-one on duty then, only the bell.'

The envelope looked similar to the last one, possibly the same. The sheet of paper inside, though, was quite different. Again the message was typed, in capitals, with no signature.

GO DOWN TO THE LORRY PARK THIS EVENING IF YOU WANT NEWS OF YOUR FRIEND.

Ruth read it several times. What silly advice, seeing as Mel was in Germany! Or maybe not. The letter didn't promise a meeting, only news.

News might be anything. It might even mean that Mel was now back in Britain. Ruth wished she'd asked Dad for the postmark date on the letter he'd received. The news might suggest more cryptic messages, through some contact Mel had in Laitheham, a secret contact who was sending these anonymous letters. But Mel had no idea Ruth was at Parkways, unless, of course, the message she'd left with Hugh Bradshaw had got through. Ruth had left the Parkways address and phone number in the hope that Melanie would ring back.

Could these letters themselves be cryptic messages if only she understood how to read them? Or was the whole idea of cryptic messages just silly, leading her astray?

In the end, Ruth decided to go to the police as she'd planned, but to call in at the lorry park on the way first.

The tide was out as she walked down the hill. Beyond the harbour wall the shifting, treacherous sands of the bay stretched away towards the thin line of the distant sea.

In the lorry park, the security lights were already blazing out to help wagons coming and going at the end of the working day, like the harbour lights once used to come on for unloading the fishing fleet. This lorry park was Laitheham's harbour now, its link with the outside world — a link with Germany! For the first time Ruth felt she knew what she was looking for.

She squeezed through the gap in the wall they'd used as children and stood in a patch of shadow alongside the loading-bay near the security compound. A couple of wagons were loading up. Large crates were being stacked in a massive soft-sided lorry, already piled high with oversized sacks, fertiliser, perhaps, or other chemicals.

The lights, the throb of the engines, the exotic liveries of some of the lorries, the smooth competence of the loaders — it was all exhilarating somehow, dousing her anxiety. As always, Ruth's mood rose as she watched the wagons moving out, into the wider world out there.

When he was doing a night haul, Dad used to let her and Melanie ride the half mile to their road end up in the cab with him and Mum used to step out for a word when he set them down.

Hidden in the shadows, Ruth studied the faces of the few passersby, hunting for that familiar mane of hair of Mel's, those dark vivid eyes. No, that was ridiculous. She wasn't going to find Mel here, only news of her.

What sort of news? Had one of these drivers perhaps seen Mel in Germany? It was stupid hoping for information on

162

the strength of one brief note from someone who wouldn't even sign their name, but instinctively she started looking for German registration plates. Or would it be better to go openly and ask at the site office? It was in the secure compound. Ruth decided to try it.

Though she stayed in the shadows, one or two of the loaders seemed to have noticed her. Maybe one of those was the news-bearer, but which one? A sense of unease prickled down Ruth's spine. She wished she hadn't come alone. If Brendan had been alive, he'd have come here with her. He was always up for anything new or exciting, just like Melanie. Had there really been a relationship between him and Mel? If so, that would mean three strings to her bow — just the picture she'd been given of her cousin at the country club.

Ruth couldn't believe it. If it was true, something terrible had happened to change the sincere, kind, caring girl she'd known all her life. But then Paul was caring and sensitive, and he had two sides to him, and Brian had lived a complete double life, unknown to her until fate brought everything to light.

Paul had laughed when she'd told him about the pranks she and Melanie had got up to here as children, happy laughter, shared secrets. Ruth wished he was here now, a rock to lean on. She no longer had misgivings about Dad being in partnership with him. Dad, she knew, would shout at her for what she was doing now. He'd call it foolhardy, and making a fool of herself, chasing after an anonymous letter! Only she was desperate for news of Mel.

There was an unmanned gate into the security compound. Ruth walked through it and found herself near the enormous soft-sider again. Crates were still being loaded into it, though the driver was already in his seat.

'Get a move on,' he yelled out to the loaders. 'I've a long haul and a ferry to catch.'

Foreign stickers were plastered all

over the cab door — Amsterdam, Prague, Berlin, Hamburg. Hamburg! Was this it? Was he the person with news of Melanie?

A voice crackled over the address system, a familiar voice, but Ruth couldn't pin it down. A man appeared on the surveillance tower, the look-out, wearing the same donkey-jacket and woolly hat as before. The hat hid half his face, a familiar face, nonetheless. Yet, again, Ruth couldn't quite pin it down. He disappeared into the tower and the voice crackled out again. A door banged and more bright lights came on.

At the front of the lorry, Ruth saw the co-driver leap up into the cab. Soon the lorry would drive away and her opportunity for news vanish. She moved forward. A transit van brought a few more crates for the soft-sider. The loaders dragged them out, then the transit van departed, lurching violently as the driver tried to pull away without releasing the handbrake!

Nerves, Ruth thought, recalling her own first attempts behind the wheel, and glanced sympathetically at the driver. To her astonishment, she recognised Rudi Leonardson! He must have turned her way and seen her just as Ruth recognised him. The smile on Ruth's face froze at the undisguised anger and menace in his eyes.

At once a mask came down and the hotel manager acknowledged her with his usual friendly wave and smile. Then he turned up his headlamps full, almost blinding her, and drove out of the complex down the road towards the hotel, like a racing driver on a track. Or like Brendan, in that beat-up old van he'd had. Ruth remembered that she'd once seen those two together here. This time Rudi Leonardson wasn't collecting goods, though — he was bringing them.

Ruth studied the wooden crates he'd brought. They were a couple of metres long, odd-looking with neither labels or firms' stencils on them. As children, instead of collecting stamps, she and

Melanie had collected the names on crates. They'd had a notebook full of them. All commercial crates had their labels and often logos, too, and even private consignments had to have a direction label.

But these crates had none at all. They were all as tall as a man, large enough to hold a man, or a woman! Large enough to hold Melanie!

With a sudden burning certainty, Ruth knew that she'd found what she'd come here to find. The anonymous letter writer hadn't led her astray. Melanie was in one of these crates.

12

The loaders heaved the three crates into the lorry then pulled down the rear, but, Ruth noticed, not bothering with the locks. The driver then started up his engine.

Ruth dashed forward and scrambled on to the back of the wagon. Keeping her balance with one hand, she gave the rear closure a sharp shove with the other. Well-oiled, it flew up at a touch. Ruth scrambled inside just as the driver started to ease forward.

In the dark inner of the lorry, she hunted round for the crates among all the other freight. Brilliant flashes of light from the security lamps through the part-open rear helped her, but the open latches might also alert bystanders and give her away. Ruth turned back to pull it down.

The lorry was now bumping out of

the entrance to the security pound on to the main hard-standing. Ruth glanced back at the inner pound. A familiar figure was hurtling across the Tarmac towards her.

'Go back, Paul!' she shouted at him. 'Get the police!'

Paul seemed to hear her voice, hesitated and raised his hand, then continued dashing towards her. The lorry slowed for the sharp turn on to the road. Paul was gaining on them, almost there. Behind him, running like a madman, Ruth saw Rudi Leonardson, shouting, but Ruth couldn't hear his words. Paul jumped for the back of the lorry, but as he did so, the lorry jerked into reverse. The unexpected impact knocked Paul as he grabbed at the rear and he fell beneath the wheels. Ruth screamed.

'Not now, my dear.'

A large hand came over her mouth and a strong arm forced her back against the lorry side. Glittering, angry eyes came into view, half-shrouded by a thick, woolly cap. It was the man Ruth had seen on the surveillance tower, the man in the donkey-jacket, the look-out.

'Just stay quiet, my dear, and no harm will come to you.'

'Doctor Roberts!'

'At your service, Miss Tamworth. I always imagined we might meet again.'

Ruth tried to struggle in his grasp, but he produced a syringe and jabbed her in the arm. She lost consciousness.

The drug held Ruth unconscious through most of the next day, when she awoke in a hospital bed. Immediately, a doctor appeared to give her an examination.

'Where am I?' Ruth asked him.

'Laitheham Cottage Hospital,' he told her, 'and seemingly not much the worse for wear.'

All the same, he left some tablets to soothe her to sleep again.

Next time she awoke, two police officers were waiting to question her. Ruth also questioned them about Paul.

'Very seriously injured, I'm afraid,'

they told her. 'They've flown him to Newcastle, actually.'

Left alone, Ruth lay a long while just thinking before she fell asleep once more. This time when she awoke, Melanie was sitting by her bed! At the sight of her, tears trickled down Ruth's cheeks. Pale, hollowed-eyed and even thinner than she used to be, Melanie's face wore a look of despair.

'What happened, Mel?' Ruth asked. 'Were you in one of those crates?'

Melanie nodded silently, the remembered nightmare darkening her eyes.

'Did I imagine it, love, or did you really leave me cryptic messages?'

'I had no other way to communicate. My ring was the first. I thought someone would find it and send it home and it'd tell you something was wrong.'

'I knew something wasn't right when they said you'd been dismissed from your job for misconduct,' Ruth said.

'I never lost my job. Nigel came and dragged me away from my flat, by force.'

'Nigel?'

'Dr Roberts, except that he isn't a real doctor. It's a syndicate and he's the head of it.'

'Did you have an affair with him, Mel?'

'Only a couple of dates, before I met Hugh.'

'Hugh Bradshaw? I went to see his family, you know.'

'Poor Mam and Eve! Nigel force-fed Hugh on drugs to change his personality. They thought I'd turn away from him then. But I love Hugh, Ruth.'

That tilt of the head was the first sign of the old Melanie. Ruth breathed a sigh of relief.

'Tell me the whole story, love.'

★ ★ ★

Ruth gave Paul a potted version of Mel's adventure when she visited him in the spinal unit at Newcastle two days later.

'Not long, mind,' the nurse warned.

172

'He's got serious injuries.'

It was a simple story, really. Nigel Roberts actually owned The Highlander. Rudi Leonardson was his second man. He owned the lorry park, with a consortium. The consortium was straight, Mel said, but Rudi, on the spot, used it to transport abroad all the valuable small equipment the gang was stealing from hospitals.

'You mean all those thefts in the newspapers this last year or two?' Paul asked.

'Nigel Roberts forged identity cards and the gang removed the items quite openly, for servicing. There's a handful of crooked lorry men willing to take special consignments in return for a fee in their back pocket.'

These special consignments had included three unnamed crates containing Melanie, Hugh and the foreign waiter from The Highlander, who'd given them Hugh's address and sent the anonymous letters in an attempt to help. He'd been badly beaten up but was expected to survive.

Poor Brendan had also been a small cog in their machine, and one that looked like giving too much away to Ruth. The gang was completely ruthless. She and Paul had asked too many questions, so they'd tried to put them out of action by rigging the car crash up on the fell road, and Ruth's fall down the stairs at Parkways, and by luring Paul back to Harleywell by false news that his aunt was dangerously ill.

Paul had smelled a rat and checked with the hospital. No-one knew what might have been waiting for him if he hadn't and found it was all a trick.

Ruth started tell Paul about Brendan, but the vigilant nurse behind the screen was tapping her watch.

'I'll tell you the rest next time,' Ruth promised. 'I'm staying in Laitheham with Melanie. She wants to be near Hugh while he's dried out. I'll come and see you every day while I'm there.'

'But that's a round trip of one hundred and sixty miles!'

'You've earned it,' she said, giving him a tender smile.

He had, after all, probably saved her life by alerting the police the minute he'd realised something was up and then returning to Laitheham and coming in search of her after noticing the anonymous letter she happened to have left in her pigeon-hole at the hotel.

Paul had a claim on her gratitude, and for everyone's sake Ruth knew she mustn't let it show that she'd willingly travel twice as far just for the happiness of sitting by his bed.

She hadn't yet seen Janice, but one day, Paul would regain the full use of his arms and legs. When he did, he'd return to his old life, and the only role she had to play in that was as his partner's daughter, the person who was going to run their Laitheham shop.

A month later, Paul was sent by ambulance to continue his treatment at Harleywell Hospital. Ruth had returned home ten days before and immediately started visiting him there. He was still heavily strapped up, so she read to him and played music to him, and even wrote replies for him to the many cards he received.

As the weeks passed, Ruth found herself keeping an eye on the craft centre for him, too, dealing with all the business requirements, all the organising that was too much for Aunt Margaret. Inevitably, after a while, she began changing the displays as well, doing things her own way.

'I like that,' Paul commented when she brought him photos of her changes in the kitchenware area.

'I got the idea from Janice's garden centre,' Ruth confessed, then bit her tongue, as Janice was something they'd not yet talked about.

'No, don't change the subject,' Paul said. 'We need to talk.'

Ruth nodded, reluctantly. Janice's part in what had happened in Laitheham wasn't a happy one, as it had turned out.

She had known Nigel Roberts was

holding Melanie and Hugh against their will, but concealed the fact. She'd also carried information to Rudi Leonardson, who'd passed it on to Nigel Roberts, giving him the means to lay the trap that lured Paul away. She'd also knowingly acted as go-between for Rudi with other members of the gang who worked at the country club, and she'd alerted Rudi about the first anonymous letter Ruth had received, putting him on his guard so that he took action to keep her out of the way.

The police had proof, apparently, that it was Rudi who'd tampered with the lights at Parkways and left the vacuum cleaner to trip her up, then blinded her with a high-powered camera flash. Flashing lights, it seemed, were a speciality of his. He'd used them on the fell road with Paul, with Ruth at Parkways, and most likely he'd used the same trick to startle Brendan into crashing his car on the quarry track.

Janice had confessed or hinted at all these things in a painful interview, of her own choosing, in Laitheham before Ruth left, and, less hysterically, in a letter to Paul. Rudi Leonardson was an enigma, a deep-dyed criminal and Nigel Roberts' right-hand man. Yet in the end, he'd given himself up and gone to the police of his own free will to save Ruth and the victims in the crates. He had a soft centre, as Brendan had once said.

'Janice says she's going to stand by Rudi,' Ruth commented, 'but it'll be a long prison sentence he receives.'

'I was never in love with Janice, Ruth.'

'She thought you were.'

'Janice just wants men to be in love with her, and imagines things mean more than they do. I took an interest in her kids, because I could see they were drifting into bad company, but Jan thought I was fishing for her.'

'I know what you mean about the twins.'

Ruth now told him what she'd seen at the club.

'I think Janice finds them a tie, in the way,' she concluded.

Paul nodded.

'And also if she feels slighted. She has a very jealous streak and lashes out.'

'She needs the security of knowing she's Number One. Rudi can give her that now, even with this long sentence ahead of him.'

'As soon as you came on the scene, Jan could see she wasn't Number One with me,' Paul went on.

Ruth stayed silent.

'You do actually realise that I'm not a man with a girl in every port, don't you, Ruth?'

Ruth glanced up and met his eyes, smiling and gentle.

'I do know it,' she replied, 'now.'

Paul's fingers, now released from their strappings, squeezed her arm.

'I was like the proverbial burned child who fears the fire, because I'd been hurt before.'

'Tell me about it.'

It was easy to tell the story now of

her engagement to Brian, with Paul's understanding eyes watching her. She told him all about the eventual quarrels when Ruth still wanted to keep some things for their wedding night. Then came Brian's secret affair and the cruel way it came to light.

'I couldn't believe it when I first read it in the newspaper. Dad couldn't either. Even Melanie couldn't, and she didn't like Brian very much.'

Paul sat silent, waiting for her to continue.

'Brian used to spend nights at this girlfriend's flat. One night there was a fire. The two of them just managed to escape, in their nightwear. There were pictures of them all over the front page of the local newspaper.'

Paul stroked Ruth's hair back from her face.

'I gave him back his ring.'

'And tried to rebuild your life?'

'I didn't actually have a broken heart, but my self-confidence had taken a terrible knock. I didn't trust anybody any more. I no longer trusted my own senses, my certainty of what someone was like behind their mask.'

'Trust is the foundation stone of love,' Paul commented.

He looked as thought to continue, but another visitor was announced, and it wasn't until Aunt Margaret finally left them alone again that they continued their conversation . . .

Soon, Paul's wheel-chair was unnecessary and he was able to get around on walking-sticks. After a while, they were also thrown aside and he returned to walking unaided on flat ground. Stairs followed, as did a return to normal life in his flat above the craft centre.

On the first day he was fit to drive again, he took Ruth to Harleywell Mere for a day out. Most of the big decisions between them had already been made. Ruth had given up her former job at the flower shop and was now permanently installed as manager at the craft centre. A contract to rent the premises Dad had found in Laitheham was signed and sealed and for the time being, Melanie was going to run the Laitheham shop, to be near Hugh until he was on his feet again.

Only one thing remained.

Against a background of ducks quacking and the gentle lapping of the mere in the reeds, Paul asked Ruth to marry him.

'You will agree to become Mrs Mackay?' he asked, with an unexpected hint of genuine anxiety in his voice.

'You know I will,' Ruth replied with a smile, and to her great surprise he eased a beautiful sapphire ring on to her finger.

The sun was shining, full of warmth although it was March and although what snow they'd had had gone, a sharp frost was still on the ground. Paul held Ruth close to him and counted his blessings. One day he'd tell her how he'd found that newspaper cutting in her drawer when he'd gone to collect Melanie's letters for her. He'd tease her about keeping a picture of him dancing with his own cousin dressed as a mermaid at a charity ball, caught off balance by a photographer friend from his student days in Leeds!

He'd tell her and confess that without finding it he would never have dared hope for a return of the love he'd felt for her from the start.

We do hope that you have enjoyed reading this large print book.

Did you know that all of our titles are available for purchase?

We publish a wide range of high quality large print books including:
Romances, Mysteries, Classics
General Fiction
Non Fiction and Westerns

Special interest titles available in large print are:
The Little Oxford Dictionary
Music Book, Song Book
Hymn Book, Service Book

Also available from us courtesy of Oxford University Press:
Young Readers' Dictionary
(large print edition)
Young Readers' Thesaurus
(large print edition)

For further information or a free brochure, please contact us at:
Ulverscroft Large Print Books Ltd.,
The Green, Bradgate Road, Anstey,
Leicester, LE7 7FU, England.
Tel: (00 44) **0116 236 4325**
Fax: (00 44) **0116 234 0205**

Other titles in the
Linford Romance Library:

DANGEROUS FLIRTATION

Liz Fielding

Rosalind thought she had her life all mapped out — a job she loved, a thoughtful, reliable fiance . . . what more could she want? How was she to know that a handsome stranger with laughing blue eyes and a roguish grin would burst into her life, kiss her to distraction and turn her world upside down? But there was more to Jack Drayton than met the eye. He offered romance, excitement, and passion — and challenged Rosalind to accept. Dared she?

ROMANTIC LEGACY

Joyce Johnson

Wedding plans in ruins, Briony Gordon immerses herself in her job as senior wine buyer at Lapwings Wine Merchants until a dramatic turn of events forces her to reconsider her future. A substantial legacy from her beloved Grandfather gives her the incentive to explore new possibilities. At Moonwarra winery in Western Australia, Briony finds feuding brothers quarrelling over the Winery's future — a future which gives her a wonderful business opportunity and where she finds true love . . .